"Mmm…"

He was watching her carefully. Waiting for what she was about to say.

But there was something else she thought she could see in his eyes. Hope?

"Skills get rusty," she murmured, "if they don't get used every once in a while."

"I've heard that." Mitch closed his eyes as he whispered the words, his breath coming out in a slow sigh.

It was Jenna's turn to swallow carefully. "Even if they are a bit rusty—" she needed to catch another breath "—it's possible to fix that. If…you know… you want to."

Mitch's eyes were open again. His gaze was fixed on Jenna's with all the intensity it had a few minutes ago before that first butterfly-wing kiss.

"Oh…I want to," he said softly. "But what about you?"

Again, Jenna stood on tiptoes, and this time, she reached up to put her hands on Mitch's cheeks to encourage him to bend his head so that she could kiss him.

"Same…"

Dear Reader,

My first career (in another life) was as a primary school teacher, but it wasn't until I became an author that my lifelong interest in the world of medicine became a real passion. I was researching a scene for an early Harlequin Medical Romance and had the opportunity to talk to a paramedic about how the ambulance service would deal with a major train crash. He invited me to go for a "ride-along" with a crew one night and it changed my life. I became a paramedic and worked both on the road and helping to train other ambulance officers.

Sometimes, all these threads of my life come together and I get to write a story that involves paramedics and doctors, frontline medicine and…classrooms and teaching. :-) My hero, Andrew "Mitch" Mitchell, goes to a training course run by the ambulance service to help rural doctors in their roles of being first responders in medical emergencies. His teacher is Jenna, but she's going to teach him more than the sessions in this course—he's going to learn that a second chance is possible for a future he thought he'd lost.

Happy reading!

Alison xx

STOLEN NIGHTS WITH THE SINGLE DAD

———

ALISON ROBERTS

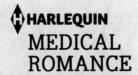

HARLEQUIN

MEDICAL
ROMANCE

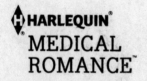

Recycling programs
for this product may
not exist in your area.

ISBN-13: 978-1-335-40865-5

Stolen Nights with the Single Dad

Copyright © 2021 by Alison Roberts

This edition published by arrangement with Harlequin Books S.A.

For questions and comments about the quality of this book,
please contact us at CustomerService@Harlequin.com.

Harlequin Enterprises ULC
22 Adelaide St. West, 40th Floor
Toronto, Ontario M5H 4E3, Canada
www.Harlequin.com

Printed in U.S.A.

Alison Roberts is a New Zealander, currently lucky enough to be living in the South of France. She is also lucky enough to write for the Harlequin Medical Romance line. A primary school teacher in a former life, she is now a qualified paramedic. She loves to travel and dance, drink champagne, and spend time with her daughter and her friends.

Books by Alison Roberts

Harlequin Medical Romance

Twins Reunited on the Children's Ward

A Pup to Rescue Their Hearts
A Surgeon with a Secret

Royal Christmas at Seattle General

Falling for the Secret Prince

Medics, Sisters, Brides

Awakening the Shy Nurse
Saved by Their Miracle Baby

Melting the Trauma Doc's Heart
Single Dad in Her Stocking
The Paramedic's Unexpected Hero
Unlocking the Rebel's Heart

Visit the Author Profile page
at Harlequin.com for more titles.

CHAPTER ONE

'ALL SET FOR TOMORROW, Mitch?'

'Almost.' Dr Andrew Mitchell looked up from where he was filing a laboratory report into a set of patient notes. 'How 'bout you, Euan? I'm sorry it's such short notice to cover my list as well as yours. I wasn't really expecting them to still have a place available on this course when I rang yesterday.'

Euan McKendry added a shrug to his smile as he stepped further into this consulting room in Allensbury's medical centre. 'It's not a problem. You're covering for me through the Christmas holidays—like you always do.' His smile widened. 'This is the first chance I've had to repay that cover.' He was beside Mitch's desk now. Close enough to pick up the glossy pamphlet that had been anchored by a plastic model of a human heart.

'Don't lose that. I need it to find where

I'm going tomorrow morning or I might get horribly lost.'

'At least it's on the south side of London. You must know the area around Croydon pretty well, given thatit's not too far from where you used to work.'

'I haven't had that much to do with the ambulance service there, though, and that's where the course is being held.'

Mitch closed the patient notes and put them to one side, going back to his computer screen to make sure the digital copy had also been filed. A bit like this picturesque village in Surrey, Allensbury Surgery and Dispensary's filing system was a mix of modern with the trusted, traditional way of doing things. And he was fine with that. It was one of the things that had drawn him back to his childhood home, after all.

'FRAME.' Euan was reading the pamphlet. 'Catchy name.'

'First Responder at Medical Emergencies.'

'I've heard about it. I thought it was a course to train people like nurses in remote areas so that they had the skills to bridge the gap until air rescue or ambulance services could get there.'

'It is.' Mitch nodded. 'There's a five-day

course for that. But they also run a two-day initiation course specifically for GPs so that we can keep up to date with skills we might not get to use that often. Like, you know, intubation or cricothyroidotomy.'

'Should be the rest of us here doing that. It's only a few years since you were running one of London's busiest emergency departments, Mitch. If anyone's up to date with critical interventions, it's you. You could be running these sessions yourself.' He was clearly peering at the bullet points covering the course material. 'Acute pulmonary oedema, anaphylaxis, management of arrhythmias. A difficult airway…'

A difficult airway.

A succinct description often used by doctors or paramedics to label anatomy or circumstances that made it challenging and sadly sometimes impossible, to ensure that someone could continue breathing if they needed a critical intervention like intubation and ventilation. A situation that was up there with the most dramatic kind of life or death crises any medic had to face.

'Hmm…' The sound was a noncommittal grunt as Mitch clicked out of various windows to close down his computer.

He knew where his colleague was tempted to take this conversation and he needed to shut it down fast. Because, even now, more than a year since it had happened, those three words could make his breath catch in his throat and he'd have to brace himself for the flashback that could replay itself in his mind in the space of a heartbeat. A montage of emotions more than actual images, the trigger almost always a faint echo of that trickle of despair down his spine when he'd known he was fighting a battle that he wasn't going to win.

That his skills hadn't been enough to save a young mother's life…

They were three words that would also make an eye-catching title for something other than a critical care workshop—a case history report in an emergency medicine journal, perhaps. The kind of article that someone like Andrew Mitchell might well have picked up and read, years ago, as he grabbed a sandwich or a cup of coffee during a break in a relentlessly busy shift as head of an emergency department in a huge, London hospital.

He could write it himself now. He probably should, in fact, as a warning for doctors who might think that working in a big city emergency department could prepare them for coping with anything, even if they'd chosen to take a completely different direction in life to live and work in a small village less than an hour's drive from the outskirts of London. He *would* write it one of these days. Just...not yet.

Everybody had told him that nobody could have won that particular battle. The post-mortem had confirmed it but that reassurance hadn't stopped the flashbacks. Or those 'what ifs...'? that always bubbled to the surface whenever the incident was mentioned. At least he was quick enough to deflect them this time and he even stood up to signal the new direction he was taking.

'You've got a good point, though,' he told Euan briskly. 'If it's as useful as I think it might be, we'll arrange for everybody else to do the course.' This thriving small town medical centre had four doctors on staff and could easily employ another one soon. Their senior practice nurse, Meg, would probably love the challenge of attending a full course herself.

'What makes you so confident it'll be that useful?' Euan raised an eyebrow. 'What can a paramedic teach someone who was an emergency medicine consultant?'

'The woman running this course is an APP—a critical care, advanced paramedic practitioner. You know, the ones that crew those single-responder vehicles or motorbikes and get to the scene before anyone else?'

Euan nodded. 'Yeah… I guess they get more experience with serious situations than any of us see in sleepy little Allensbury.'

'Not only that…the whole initiative is the brainchild of the instructor who's running this particular course and when I rang to book in, I was told that I was super lucky because Jenna Armstrong is the best. She's the senior instructor for FRAME nationwide. She trains the trainers.'

'Sounds formidable.' Euan was grinning. 'What's the bet she's in her fifties, single and built like a battleship?'

Mitch laughed. 'I couldn't care less as long as she's good at her job.' He reached to take the pamphlet out of Euan's hands. 'I've got to get going. I promised Ollie we'd have hamburgers and chips for dinner tonight at the Riverside pub and then we both need an early night. I'll have to be on the road by seven a.m. at the latest for the next couple of mornings.'

'You could always stay in town for a night or two. Your dad's there for Ollie, isn't he? Like he is when you're on call at night?'

'Of course.' But it was Mitch's turn to shrug as he slipped the pamphlet into his laptop bag. 'But I don't want to change his routine any more than I have to. Having his grandpa look after him for a few hours here and there is a lot different to having his dad vanish for two days. He's just started school and that's enough change for a four-year-old to cope with for the next few weeks at least.'

Euan blew out a breath. 'They complicate life, don't they? Kids?'

'It's worth it.' Mitch could feel a smile tugging at the corners of his mouth. He could feel a squeeze around his heart at the same time that was sending a warmth into every cell in his body. 'You'll find out one of these days.'

'Not me.' Euan was shaking his head as he followed Mitch out of the room. 'No, thank *you*.'

How could someone be *that* sure about something as huge as turning your back on ever having a family of your own?

Mitch had to swallow a rather large lump in his throat as he looked down at the spiky black hair of the small boy who'd fallen asleep, cuddled up to him, as he listened to the story he'd been reading. It felt as though his heart could actually burst with the amount of love he had for this child and that made his movements even more gentle as he slipped his arm free from beneath Ollie, tucked the duvet securely around his son and stooped to press a kiss onto that soft hair, gently enough not to wake him, inhaling that familiar and delicious smell of baby shampoo that never seemed to fade completely between washes.

Avoiding the creaky board in front of the chest of drawers was so automatic he didn't even notice he was doing it but then everything about this small room tucked into a corner of the upper level of this rambling, old house was as familiar as the back of his own hand. Mitch had been sleeping in this room when he'd been Ollie's age. He'd never lived anywhere else, in fact, until he'd headed off to university and then medical school.

He paused by the windows to draw the curtains enough to close the gap in the middle and keep out any draughts and caught a glimpse of the garden below. His father was outside, patiently waiting for Jet, their sixteen-year-old black Labrador, to finish a slow perimeter patrol of the property and people he needed to protect.

Mitch knew as well as Jet exactly what was out there, beyond the garden gate. A narrow street filled with solid, red brick houses like this one, with its tall chimneys and the hidden garden out the back. Some of them were whitewashed and half-timbered like the old dwelling that had been converted into the medical centre and some still had thatched roofs. Allensbury was one of the Surrey villages that always made the list of 'must see' attractions not too far from London with its pretty streets, welcoming pubs, stone churches, a village square with a weekend market and the quiet river with its tree-lined banks. The surrounding forest was a little wilder but just as familiar to Mitch as this house and his childhood bedroom had been.

That familiarity that felt like safety—like *home*—had been the reason he'd turned his life upside down and come back here.

No…that wasn't true, was it? His world

had already been well and truly turned upside down before he'd had to admit defeat and give up on the lifestyle and career that had been a dream come true. If he had known what was coming—the brutal rollercoaster of just a few, short days in which his son had been born but he'd lost his wife—would he have chosen to go down that path? Or would he have been just as emphatic as Euan in vowing that it wasn't for him?

Maybe he would have been. Who, in their right mind, would ever put their hand up to experience that kind of pain? That lump was back in his throat as he took one more glance at Ollie's face, bathed in the soft glow from his dinosaur nightlight, dark lashes fluttering on pale cheeks as his dreams captured him.

It was just as well Mitch had never been given that choice, then, because he would never have known just how much it was possible to love a small human. How, from that first moment of holding his tiny son in his arms, he'd discovered a new form of love that could actually change how you viewed the entire world, including the new appreciation for the love of his own parent. Sadly, he'd lost his mum years before but his dad,

Michael—along with his childhood home and even Jet the dog–had been the anchor he'd badly needed in a world that had suddenly gone so very, very wrong.

His small family had been his absolute priority in those darkest of days. The only thing that had really mattered.

It still was.

She'd noticed him the instant she'd walked into the classroom.

It wasn't simply that he was an extremely good-looking man. Jenna Armstrong had been immune to surface attraction like that for too many years to count now. No...there was something else about him. Something she couldn't quite define. Maybe it was the way he was sitting, with those long limbs relaxed enough to suggest it would be difficult to find an environment that would intimidate him but with an aura of energy that contradicted any laid-back impression. This was a man who looked as if he could take command of any situation in the space of a finger-click.

'Welcome, everybody,' she said, putting the box of handouts she'd just finished printing onto a desk in the corner of the room.

'I'm Jenna and we've got a busy couple of days ahead of us as I take you through our FRAME initiation course for doctors.'

She moved to close a window as the sound of a siren being activated just beneath them startled everybody enough to turn their heads. Everybody except the man at the back, she noticed.

'Sorry about that. This is a busy ambulance station so we'll get a bit of that kind of disruption but the resources we have here make this an ideal training space.' She smiled at the group. 'It might also remind us of why we're here. I know that you're all doctors with your own busy practices so I want to thank you for taking the time to join this programme and become a valuable extension to emergency ambulance services. You'll leave here with a specialised kit including the latest technology we have available, for example, a video laryngoscope that can make the difference in a difficult intubation but, more importantly, you'll leave with the skills you need to use it and any rust brushed off other skills you might not use on a regular basis.'

She had the attention of every one of the dozen or so people in this room but Jenna could feel a particular intensity coming from that man at the back. It was an effort not to let her gaze get immediately drawn back to him but, for some reason, that intensity was oddly disturbing.

'Bit of housekeeping before we start,' she continued. 'Toilets are out the door to the left and you'll find the fire escape there as well. Food and drinks will be supplied for breaks and lunch and, please, if you go outside, stay within the red lines by the buildings. As you can tell by how early the sirens go on, some of our crews are very keen to get to a Code Blue priority call and it wouldn't be a good look if anyone on a FRAME course got squashed by an ambulance. Now…let's do a quick round robin, to get started. We'll introduce ourselves, say where we're from and maybe why we're here?'

Her smile widened. 'I'll start. I'm Jenna Armstrong, a critical care paramedic. I live not far from this station in south London and I'm here because I'm passionate about this course. I started developing it quite a few years ago and I've been all over the country getting it up and running. It's been going long enough now for statistics to confirm that it's one of the most effective strategies we've put in place to save lives in more remote areas. It's something I'm very proud of. And it's something that I can promise has the potential to make an important difference to you—and to the communities that you care for.'

There was a moment's silence when she finished speaking. Had she sounded a bit over the top? Too passionate? But it was hard not to, when this had been the total focus of her life for so long.

The only thing that had really mattered for so long.

It didn't take long to get around the group. Jenna ticked names off her list as they introduced themselves. Melanie, Ravi and Judith had come from as far away as rural areas near Basingstoke and Brighton. There were older doctors, like Peter and Jack, who felt they were getting rusty on emergency procedures and young GPs, like Susie and Indira, who were nervous about being so far away from major hospitals and advanced ambulance services. It wasn't deliberate, but the man at the back was the last person to introduce himself.

'I'm Mitch,' he said, quietly. 'I'm one of

four GPs in the only medical centre in Allensbury, which is a small town in Surrey.'

Jenna was frowning at the sheet of paper in front of her. Mitch? The only person who wasn't ticked off was an Andrew. Then she noticed his surname and almost smiled because it fitted him so well to go by a shortened version of Mitchell.

Because it was just that bit different?

'I'm here because I think we get so caught up in the ordinary busyness of general practice that we can miss opportunities to keep up to date,' Mitch said. 'And…you never know—that one skill we got rusty in might be the one skill we absolutely need to save someone's life.'

His voice was deep enough to be a bit like his body language and how he looked. Unusually attractive. Calm and confident but…somehow contradictory? Was it Jenna's imagination or was there something he wasn't saying, here?

It had only been polite to look up from the paper that listed the expected attendees for the course and meet this man's gaze as he continued speaking but it was suddenly difficult to break that eye contact.

Because she felt like she recognised what was different about him.

He was searching for something.

Something of personal significance.

And…disturbingly enough to send a tiny chill down Jenna's spine, it felt like she might have been singled out as the only person who could help him find what it was he was searching for.

CHAPTER TWO

JENNA ARMSTRONG WASN'T someone that would stand out in a crowd.

She wasn't tall—Mitch guessed a few inches over five feet, which would mean the top of her head wouldn't even reach his shoulder. She was also slim and fine-featured, which probably made her look a lot younger than she actually was. Or maybe that was partly due to the very short hair-style, which made him think of a curly version of Ollie's soft spikes that had a mind of their own when it came to being tamed.

Any ability to vanish into a crowd physically, however, was more than compensated for by an astonishing...what was it, exactly? Her *presence*? There was a confidence about her. He might have put that down to the crisp uniform she was wearing but, in fact, you could actually feel the passion that she had, not only for her work as a highly skilled paramedic but for sharing her knowledge and skills by teaching. She was a natural teacher, too. She had this entire class in the palm of her hand within minutes of completing the introductory hoops of learning each other's names and the overview of the course they were enrolled in.

There was a sense of drama as Jenna rolled down the blinds on the windows and dimmed the lights in the room to show a short video on a large screen. A dramatic footage that had to be a clip from a movie. An historical setting, judging by the clothing worn, so it had little relevance to contemporary life but it still made Mitch's blood run cold. Because it had someone riding a horse. Flying through an idyllic countryside, galloping over flower-studded fields and jumping rustic wooden gates and… he knew what was coming.

He was braced for the moment the music changed to become far more sinister and the filming went into slow motion as the horse caught its leg on a fallen log and both horse and rider somersaulted through the air before the shocking collisions with the ground that made everybody watching wince. It made Mitch close his eyes and take a slow breath in. By the time he opened his eyes again, the camera was panning out from above the scene. The horse got to its feet, stood still for a moment and then took off at a gallop.

The rider remained completely motionless and there was no sign of life as the image got smaller and smaller, until that lifeless looking person was no more than a speck in an endless—and apparently deserted—rural landscape.

There was a long moment's silence before Jenna began speaking and it was then that Mitch really heard her voice for the first time. He could hear the faint accent that might be a touch of Welsh background but, more than that, he could hear the tone of someone who knew exactly what they were doing and why.

'The horse jumps another fence and gets onto a road. Someone has the sense to go looking for the rider and then calls for help as soon as they see them lying in the field. The call taker in the emergency response centre looks up the co-ordinates and pinpoints the location of the accident on a map. They look for the nearest ambulance that might be available in the area but it's miles away—being used to transport a patient to the nearest hospital big enough to have a catheter laboratory that can deal with an evolving myocardial infarction. There's no helicopter immediately available, either, but the system flags that there's is a FRAME doctor in a nearby village medical centre, so they activate that call first.'

Jenna's voice was soft but as clear as a bell and just as captivating.

'Your pager goes off,' she tells them. 'You apologise to the patients in your waiting rooms who'll have to wait a while longer, grab your backpack kit and jump into your car. You're at the scene within minutes. And—' the pause was dramatic '—right now, you're the only medically qualified person there and you've got the gear in your pack that could tip the balance between life and death. You need to identify the critical actions that are needed urgently to prevent someone's condition from deteriorating to the point of them becoming a fatality. It's up to you to do whatever you can to save this life.'

Mitch didn't have to imagine what that would be like. He knew, only too well, how huge that sense of responsibility seemed. How powerful the determination to win was and how crushing the weight of failure could be. He also knew that their instructor couldn't possibly have deliberately chosen a scenario that was so close to the bone for him that it felt like a physical blow but that didn't help. He could feel his fingers tightening into fists as he took another deep, slow breath and fought the urge to head outside for some fresh air to clear his head as the blinds on the windows were lifting again.

This was what he'd come here for, after all. A way to revisit that nightmare and find answers to some of those 'what ifs' that might stop the fear of it happening again haunting him for the rest of his life. And he was clearly in the right place.

It almost felt as if this course had been designed specifically for him.

Maybe he wasn't hiding his reaction as well as he thought he was because Jenna turned her head to catch his gaze at that moment and there was a tiny frown between her eyes.

Brown eyes, he noticed, as the light from the windows caught them. But not as dark as his own. More a golden, hazel kind of brown. Warm eyes. Empathetic. They only held his gaze for a heartbeat and, while he had the odd feeling that she could see far more than he would have chosen to show, he didn't mind.

Because it felt like he was being understood rather than judged. As if Jenna Armstrong knew what it was like to fight that kind of battle.

And lose…

Wow…

A dramatic opening to a session on critical interventions for a FRAME doctor on scene always got everybody on board but that expression on Mitch's face meant that Jenna was the one being sucked into this scenario now—as if she could see what was happening from the point of view of the injured person and Mitch was the hero who was about to do whatever it took to save her life.

And he would, wouldn't he? Even in a split second of eye contact, she could sense just how hard he would try. How important it was to him to care for others and…she had to suck in a quick breath as she broke that contact. There was a pull here that was inexplicable and too strong to feel remotely comfortable.

'Okay…' She kept her tone brisk. Urgent,

even. 'What's the first thing that's going to kill someone the fastest?'

'An occluded airway,' Ravi offered.

Jenna nodded. 'Absolutely.' She tapped the keyboard in front of her and the first slide of a presentation filled the screen. 'One of our sessions tomorrow is going to cover identifying and managing risks on scene and whether a major incident activation is warranted but, for the moment, we're going to assume that our scene is safe and risks are controlled so we can focus on the immediate threats to life. And yes, it goes back to the basic ABCs that you will all be very familiar with. The occluded airway could be as simple as someone who's unconscious and unable to lift their chin off their chest.'

The picture on the screen now was of a car accident, the deeply unconscious driver still held upright by the safety belt but with his head flopped forward far enough to easily cut off any air entry. Jenna clicked again and this time the image was a more confronting illustration of a serious face and neck injury. 'It could also be as complex as this kind of blunt force or crush injury to the face and/ or the neck that has distorted the anatomy and rapidly continues to deteriorate due to bleeding and swelling.'

She could feel the focus with which Mitch was listening to her speak. The way he was watching her. It could have come across as creepy but it didn't. If anything, it was giving her a strange sort of internal tingle—as if he might be interested in *her* rather than what she was saying? She shook the sensation off. 'Indicators of airway compromise?'

The responses came quickly.

'Stridor.'

'Cyanosis. Or pallor.'

'No chest wall movement to be seen. Or felt.'

Mitch was the last to contribute. 'Accessory muscle use,' he said. 'Like intercostal retractions or a tracheal tug. And agitation,' he added quietly. 'Fear, even...'

There was a collective pause. This had just become rather more significant than simply discussing the theory of a medical examination. This was about people. Possibly terrified people. Somehow, it came as no surprise that it was Mitch who had made signs and symptoms something they could all relate to on a human level rather than reciting a paragraph from a medical textbook.

Jenna spoke into that moment's silence. 'You all know the list. And you all know what we need to do. Which is?'

'Open the airway,' Judith said.

'Head tilt, chin lift.' One of the younger doctors, Indira, nodded. 'And then we can move on to reassessing the respiratory efforts.'

'You're not going to do that if there's any suspicion of a spinal injury,' Jack said. 'And, if we're using that example of the horse-riding accident, that would be top of my list.'

'In that case, of course we'd use a modified jaw thrust.' Indira shook her head. 'Basic first aid, isn't it? And an occluded airway is going to kill someone faster than a potential spinal injury, isn't it? I believe it's only about ten percent of unconscious trauma patients that do have a C spine injury.'

Jenna intervened before the discussion could go off track.

'Basic first aid can very well be life-saving,' she said calmly. 'A lot of what this course is about is reminding us of things we might not have used in a long time. I think Mitch hit the nail on the head with what he said about why he had come to this course—

that one skill that we're a bit rusty in might be the one that we need, if not to save a life, then possibly to prevent making an injury a whole lot worse. I agree with you, Indira, in that making sure there's a patent airway can take precedence over anything else depending on circumstances, but I also agree with you, Jack—in the mechanism of injury like coming off a horse at high speed, a spinal injury would be well up my list as well.' She glanced around the group. 'Out of interest, who has done a modified jaw thrust recently?'

Nobody put their hand up or nodded their head. Jenna walked a few steps to the full-body mannequin that was lying on the floor at the front of the classroom.

'Let's have a quick demo.' She looked around the room but she already knew where her glance was going to stop this time. 'Mitch? You up for it?'

'Sure.'

He was taller than she'd realised. By the time he'd joined her at the front of the room, Jenna could tell that the top of her head would barely reach his shoulder. She noticed the faded, denim jeans that clung to his long legs and the soft shirt with the top buttons casually open and the sleeves rolled up almost to his elbows to reveal well-defined muscles beneath tanned skin. It was impossible not to notice the way he moved, too—with a grace that belied his height and muscle mass. The errant thought that he was probably an excellent dancer came from nowhere and was entirely inappropriate.

Without looking directly at Jenna, Mitch knelt in front of the mannequin's head. He put his hands on each side of the face, with his thumbs on the cheekbones and his fingers hooked under the angle of the jawbone. Pressing down with his thumbs and pulling up with his fingers moved the jaw without changing the line of the head or neck.

'Perfect,' Jenna announced.

Mitch got to his feet in another fluid movement and, this time, he did catch Jenna's gaze for a moment before heading back to his seat, his lips tilting into an embryonic smile as he acknowledged her commendation. The corners of a pair of very dark brown eyes crinkled a little at the same time, which made the almost smile as genuine as a wide grin might have been.

For just another moment, Jenna watched him walk away, aware of that tingle she'd dismissed not long ago. But this time it was even stronger and she could recognise it for exactly what it was.

Attraction.

The kind of attraction she hadn't felt in for ever.

Well, not exactly for ever but certainly not since she'd lost Stefan and eight years could definitely feel like for ever. She'd never expected to feel it again, either, but there it was.

Very much alive and kicking.

Nobody could have the faintest idea what had just flashed through her head but Jenna took a sharp inward breath and lifted her chin, anyway. This might be totally unexpected but it wasn't anything she couldn't deal with. She dealt with far more difficult things on a regular basis, after all.

'Right…' Her smile was bright. 'We've got that airway open. What are some of the adjuncts we might use to secure it?'

Jenna picked up a tray of items that included a hard, plastic oropharyngeal airway, a soft nasopharyngeal tube, a laryngeal mask airway and kits for more invasive airway management like tracheal intubation, needle cricothyroidotomy and surgical airways. She deliberately turned to the opposite side of the classroom from where Mitch had just taken his seat again and offered the tray to Jack.

'Pick one,' she invited. 'Tell us what it is, the indications for using it and whether it's something you carry in your own first response kit. Later today, we'll be using all of them in a practical session but, if you've used one recently yourself, tell us about that case.'

It was going to take some time to get to Mitch's side of the classroom and, by then, Jenna was quite confident she would be able to interact with him in exactly the same way she had interacted with hundreds and hundreds of students over the last few years. There was no real reason why Andrew Mitchell should be any different.

No reason at all.

The last session of the first day was a workshop. The large classroom had been rearranged to provide stations equipped with mannequins and all the gear needed to refresh skills that hadn't been used recently enough or to learn new ones. Jenna moved between where class members were working alone or in pairs, helping them to smooth over rough points or challenging them to try new techniques. Voices were quiet and the atmosphere one of intense concentration, despite a background weariness after a long and intense day of both academic and practical instruction.

This was the highlight of Mitch's day. He had a video laryngoscope in his hands for the first time in years and he could see an impressive improvement in the technology. There was a light source and a digital camera built into the tip of the laryngoscope blade and a small screen attached to the side of the sleek, easy-to-hold handle. This screen provided an enlarged view of the larynx and all the anatomical landmarks you were looking for in order to pass a breathing tube into the trachea and secure an airway. With his other hand, he was following the angle of the blade to slip the tip of the stylet, loaded with the endotracheal tube, through the vocal cords and into the trachea. He then needed to advance the tube and remove the stylet.

That was when the process stopped going so smoothly.

Mitch could feel the hairs on the back of his neck prickle as he felt the resistance beneath his fingers. It was all too easy to imagine that this was a real emergency situation—maybe even the last chance to secure an airway before his patient ran into the life-threatening complications that came from a prolonged lack of oxygen. He tried again but still couldn't advance the tube.

What the hell was going on? Was this a crisis in confidence because the last time he'd needed to use this skill had been such a catastrophe? Had he lost an ability that had been a strength he had relied on more times than he could ever have counted?

He felt, rather than saw, someone coming to stand by his shoulder and he knew, beyond any shadow of doubt, that it was Jenna Armstrong—not just because she was running this workshop and making a point of coaching everybody, but because he could feel that…presence she had. The calmness. Confidence. Empathy…?

Whatever. She was the last person that Mitch wanted to watch him fail. He might have even sworn softly, under his breath.

Jenna's voice was quiet. She didn't seem the least bothered by the difficulty he was in.

'Good to see you've found the downside of this new breed of stylet,' she said. 'The angle of the curve is sharper than we've used in the past. It mirrors the angle of the video laryngoscope's blade, which is good but it makes it harder to advance the tube once you've got the tip through the cords. Try popping the stylet off with your thumb, back it out a bit and then try advancing the tube.'

And, just like that, it was suddenly easy. Mitch slid the tube into place, removed the stylet completely and attached the syringe to the balloon valve, inflating it with enough air to secure it within the trachea. Then he covered the mannequin's mouth and nose with the mask and squeezed the bag. It was so much easier to watch exposed, pink plastic lungs rather than putting his stethoscope onto a real person to check correct tube positioning by watching and listening to see if the air entry was equal on both sides.

'Cool…' The praise from his instructor was matter-of-fact. 'Now…start again.'

He glanced sideways. Were there enough of the video laryngoscopes for everybody to be getting a chance to practise this much? Tomorrow afternoon would be an assessment scenario and they would all be expected to discuss and demonstrate the use of emergency procedures like this before being signed off as FRAME practitioners. He didn't want to monopolise this station.

But Jenna met his glance steadily.

As if she *knew* how important this was to him.

Silently, he removed the tube from the mannequin and set everything up to do it again. He didn't mind Jenna watching this time. Quite the opposite. Especially when he heard the tiny hum of approval she made.

'You've had a lot of experience with intubation, yes?'

'Mmm.' Mitch was focused on the screen. 'Used to work in an ED,' he told her, casually. She didn't need to know that he'd been the head of that department, did she? And it was part of a life he'd left behind so it wasn't even relevant. 'It's a lot different in general practice,' he added. 'I'm planning to seriously upgrade our emergency kits. Video laryngoscopes. Flexible endoscopes. If only…' He trailed into silence, having already said more than he'd intended.

'If only you'd had one of them on a difficult case?' Jenna's voice was quiet. 'I have to admit that I got the feeling there's a story behind why you came on this course.'

'Yeah…' Mitch could see the vocal cords

on the screen now. He could push the stylet and tube through but his hand had stilled.

'We've all got "if only" cases,' Jenna said. 'I've got a few of my own.'

'But you wouldn't get the children coming into your surgery.' Mitch swallowed hard. 'Three little kids who are growing up without their mum because it wasn't possible to give her an airway.'

'And you think having a video laryngoscope would have made the difference?'

'They said not. Post-mortem results showed a laryngeal fracture, a C3/4 fracture *and* cord damage so even if she had survived, she would have been tetraplegic.'

'Sounds like a very nasty accident. What was she doing?'

Mitch's gaze flicked up. 'Riding her horse. Jumping cross country. She was one of our local equestrian stars and she was training for last year's three-day event at Burghley.'

He saw the way Jenna's pupils dilated. Heard the sharp intake of her breath. 'Oh…' There was no need for her to say that she understand exactly what a gut-punch her introductory video must have been. 'I'm so sorry, Mitch.'

'You weren't to know. It was a good reminder of why I'd come.' Mitch turned back to his task and, this time, it was a smooth process to get the tube into place and secure it. He was reaching for the bag mask when Jenna spoke again, quietly enough for him to know that these words were only for him to hear.

'They say so much, don't they? Or hide it. Those two little words. "If only". Or "what if"?'

Mitch had two fingers under the mannequin's jawbone to help hold the mask on firmly. He inflated the bag and watched the lungs fill with air. 'They do.'

'I find they can blindside you in the most unexpected moments.' Jenna's voice wasn't much more than a murmur. Certainly none of the other people in this room would be hearing this private conversation.

'And keep you awake in the tiny hours of the night,' Mitch agreed.

'They're not necessarily a bad thing, though. As long as you don't let them take too much away from what's important in your life.'

He didn't need to inflate the lungs again but he did. Slowly. Without even thinking about what he was doing, because he was wondering what kind of things kept Jenna Armstrong awake at night or blindsided her when she least expected it. What was even more curious was how much he wanted to know. How interested he was in this woman...

'And they can be a very good thing,' Jenna added. 'When they make you grab them with both hands and shake them until an answer falls out, they can be life-changing.'

Mitch looked up again in time to see Jenna's lips curving into a smile.

'Like you coming on this course,' she told him. 'Becoming someone that'll be registered on the emergency services system and able to be responded fast to critical situations—with the best kit we can supply.'

'Jenna?' Judith was calling from the other side of the room. 'I'm having trouble with this video thingy.'

'Coming...' But Jenna didn't move for a moment. She was still holding Mitch's gaze. 'Think about that the next time you're doing the "if only" game. Think about how the changes you're making now might affect future cases. How many lives that might get saved because you're doing this.'

Mitch watched her walking over to where

Judith was working. He needed to tidy up this station and move on himself because he probably had time to practise with the crico-thyroidotomy mannequin before he needed to hit the road and battle rush hour traffic to get home.

But he stayed very still for a moment longer.

Watching Jenna.

Letting it sink in that the brief, almost whispered conversation he'd just had with Jenna had done something that might have just lifted the remnants of the significant weight he'd been carrying on his shoulders for the last year.

It was such a cliché to think in terms of a silver lining to a cloud or some such rubbish but there was definitely something profound that Jenna's words had left him with and…it did feel like coming on this course might be going to mark a changing point in his life. A positive change.

'Ah…coffee…'

'Here, have this one.' Susie was already pouring a mug of coffee from the table set up at the back of their classroom. 'You look like you need it more than I do, Mitch.'

'Early start. And I got home pretty late. The traffic was appalling yesterday evening.'

'I got the train. Bit of a walk from the station to get home but I rather like that. The calm before the storm.' Susie was smiling as she handed him a steaming mug. 'Milk?'

'No, thanks. Black's good.'

'Storm?' Jenna queried as she joined them. She picked up two mugs and handed one to Susie.

'Circus might be a better description. You know—husband, kids and the dog all demanding attention?'

Jenna shook her head. 'No. I don't have to cope with any of that. Thank goodness. Good for you, fitting in this course on top of your work and home commitments like that on top. I couldn't do it.'

Mitch stepped back to one side, sipping his coffee as more people arrived and headed their way. The tone of her voice when she'd said 'Thank goodness' made it sound as if a husband and kids were the last thing she would want in her life.

Judith had heard the exchange between Susie and Jenna. 'You do far more, from what I heard. Someone told me yesterday that you've written a book? A textbook for paramedics?'

'It kind of grew from the first set of clinical guidelines I helped write when the FRAME initiative was set up.' Jenna's shrug was modest. 'And they need updating already, which is an extra project I've got on at the moment. Things change, as you'll all be well aware of—like the emergency management of heart attacks and now occlusive strokes by thrombolysis in the field.'

'You travel all around the country with your teaching, as well.' Susie's tone was admiring. Or possibly envious?

'Not so much these days. We're getting a great cohort of instructors based in various cities. In the early days, I was hardly ever at home. I couldn't have done my job if I'd had a dog, let alone a whole family, like you, Susie.'

'But you love it.' Mitch's quiet comment wasn't a question. She hadn't needed to tell them all how much she loved her job yesterday because it had been so obvious. The passion she had for her career gave her a glow that made it hard to look away from her.

Especially when she smiled like that.

'I do,' she agreed. 'I'm particularly loving

the work on the new clinical guidelines—which you'll all receive in the mail as soon as they're completed, by the way. We've got a great team of experts on board, including emergency department consultants and specialists from cardiology, neurology and orthopaedics, to name just a few. It's exciting.'

'And you still find time to work on the road,' Judith said. 'I can't even get round to weeding my garden.'

'I need to keep my own skills current,' Jenna said. 'I'd feel like a complete fraud teaching a course like this if I didn't. Especially when I've got a group of doctors who already know more than I do.'

'Are you kidding?' Susie raised her eyebrows. 'I spend half my days writing repeat prescriptions and trying to convince people that they'd feel a lot better if they stopped smoking and lost a bit of weight. I've never used a laryngeal mask airway and I have to confess, the thought of having to perform a cricothyroidotomy on a real patient is terrifying. Wrangling three overtired kids into bed is a breeze in comparison. Especially when the husband gives me a hand like he did last night.'

Mitch closed his eyes as he took another

sip of his coffee. Ollie hadn't gone to sleep at his usual time yesterday so he'd been over-tired by the time Mitch had got home as well, but how lucky were they both that there was a loving grandparent on hand and bath time had clearly been a joy for both of them.

'I waited for you, Daddy,' Ollie had said kindly. *'I knew you'd want your goodnight kiss...'*

And that feeling, when those small arms got wound tightly around his neck—that feeling of being *home*…

Mitch wouldn't give that up, no matter how exciting a career it could allow. He'd done the opposite, in fact, hadn't he? He could have been one of those experts on the team Jenna was working with to produce those updated clinical guidelines. He'd had the fastest-paced, most challenging job ever, running that hectic emergency department, but he'd given it up for his son and he'd do the same again in a heartbeat.

'Well, you have my respect,' Jenna told Susie. 'I think you're juggling a lot more than I do.'

'It's worth it,' Judith said quietly. 'My lot have grown up and left home now but you know what? I can't wait for the grandkids to start arriving. I kind of miss that chaos and clutter.' She smiled. 'I won't have to wait too long, either. My daughter's pregnant. Due in a few weeks. It hasn't been an easy pregnancy so we're both looking forward to the birth.'

Nobody could miss that look that passed between Judith and Susie. The understanding of one mother to another. Mitch could have nodded his own agreement that parenting was worth any struggle but, for some reason, he didn't. Because he was watching Jenna's reaction, closely enough to catch a flash of something that caught his attention. Gave his heart a bit of squeeze, to be honest. It looked like she'd lost something and it made him wonder if she'd wanted kids and had found she couldn't have them for some reason. Or if she'd lost the person she'd wanted to have them *with*.

The impression was gone in a blink, however, and Jenna was smiling now.

'I wasn't kidding when I was banging on yesterday about how much I love my job,' she said. 'It's everything to me and I'm not about to let anything get in the way of being able to give it everything I've got. It's not that I don't like kids. I love them.' Her smile widened. 'As long as they get to go home with someone else.' She was already turning away. 'We'd better get cracking. We've got a lot to get through today.'

The stimulating effects of the strong coffee had probably worn off by the time they were into the second session of the morning but Mitch still felt alert enough to be absorbing—and enjoying—everything he was listening to Jenna saying about eye injuries that were considered to be emergencies due to their life-changing potential loss of vision.

'So the usual cause of an orbital floor fracture is when a blunt object, of equal or greater diameter than the orbital aperture, strikes the eye.' Jenna grinned at her class. 'And one of the reasons I love talking about them is that we get to use really cool words when we're discussing the signs and symptoms. Okay…quick quiz. What's diplopia?'

'Double vision,' Peter answered.

'Ecchymosis?'

'Black eye.' It was Melanie who responded first this time.

'Ipsilateral epistaxis?'

'Nose bleed on one side only,' Indira said.

Jenna was nodding at each correct answer and clicking a remote control to bring up a corresponding image as confirmation. The quiz was rapid and the class members— including Mitch—were clearly enjoying the participation.

He was enjoying more than the quiz, however. The feeling that something had changed yesterday, after that brief, private conversation with Jenna, had not worn off. If anything, it was stronger now and Mitch was feeling a lot more relaxed. As if he'd somehow absorbed some of the serenity that came from the combination of passion and knowledge that gave Jenna that very appealing glow?

Maybe it was the idea that you could look back on even catastrophic events and realise that they were the catalyst for something good that wouldn't have otherwise happened. Like him coming on this course and putting himself on the front line for local emergency service call-outs. There was a frisson of excitement to be found in the idea that his world would be expanding to include some of the things he thought he'd left far behind in his career but there was something deeper as well. The idea that he was changing more than an element of his working life? That he might become a better doctor because of this? A better person, even?

'Traumatic hyphaema?'

There was a longer pause before anyone answered this time. Mitch knew the answer but he was momentarily distracted as he watched the way Jenna caught one corner of her bottom lip between her teeth as she waited. She was loving challenging these doctors and that glow had just ramped up a notch or two.

Good Lord…had he really thought that this woman would not stand out in a crowd because of how she looked? Her intelligence was shining just as brightly and Mitch already knew how compassionate Jenna was. How empathetic. She'd known exactly how horrific it must have been for him to watch that dramatic accident scene involving a fall from a horse. He'd also been left with the impression that she more than understood what it was like to lie awake half the night being tortured by thoughts of how different things could have been.

'Is it blood in the anterior chamber of the eye?' Jack sounded a little hesitant as he broke the silence in the classroom.

'Yes…excellent!' The image that came onto the screen of a close-up shot of blood obscuring even the iris of an eye was enough to make a couple of people groan but Jenna was obviously happy as she clicked through more images and talked more about the implications of the sign.

But Mitch was still watching her rather than the screen.

If he had been looking for another woman in his life—which he wasn't—then Jenna would have been perfect.

Apart from that one little detail he'd learned over coffee this morning that meant she was actually the absolute opposite of perfect, of course. If he was ever going to share his life with a partner again, he'd have to find someone who not only loved him but would love his child as her own. The fear of risking Ollie's happiness in any way was so abhorrent it had been more than enough to let Mitch close the door firmly on even thinking about looking for someone.

Not that he'd needed an extra incentive to not get too close to anyone again. He'd loved Tegan. So much. And he'd known for a very long time that that part of his heart had died along with his wife. It was a no-brainer that he could never love another woman in a way that was fearlessly based on the confidence that they had the rest of a normal lifespan to be together. Even if that gaping hole in his heart had somehow, miraculously healed itself, he wouldn't *want* to offer that much of himself to someone else. He didn't even want to try dating anyone to try and find out how much of a relationship might be possible.

He couldn't afford to get broken again. Not when he had his precious son to raise.

But that didn't mean he didn't miss the sexual side of a relationship, did it? It wasn't normal for someone in his stage of life to be living like a monk, although it had seemed relatively easy up until now. Maybe that was why he was finding this unexpected attraction to Jenna rather disturbing. And maybe he could find a way to add the perfectly normal pleasure of sex back into his life at some point.

No...he had to dismiss that notion as he refocused on what was happening around him. A casual arrangement for a friendship with benefits would never work when he had a small child and worked in a small town. It was much safer for everybody for him to just focus on his life as a parent and his work as a GP. A life that was about to get more challenging and no doubt satisfying by him becoming qualified as a FRAME practitioner.

'Okay, last one…' Jenna's tone suggested it might also be the hardest. 'Enophthalmos?' Her grin was cheeky. 'And, yes—that does have two 'h's in it.'

Her gaze roamed over her silent students before finally resting on Mitch. The remnants of that grin were still evident in the curve of her lips and he couldn't help smiling back.

'It's a posterior displacement of a normal-sized globe in relation to the bony orbital margin,' he said. 'Or, more simply, a sinking of the eyeball into the orbital cavity.'

'Just what I was about to say.'

Judith's wry comment made everybody laugh, including Jenna, but the look she was giving Mitch was not one of amusement. He'd impressed her, hadn't he? And he rather liked that.

Okay…he liked it a lot.

He liked *her* a lot.

And…and maybe the fact that she was the total opposite of a woman he'd choose to have as part of his life wasn't a bad thing.

She'd feel exactly the same way about him, surely? With the way she felt about kids, a single father would be a nightmare scenario. But what if Jenna's incredibly busy career meant that she was as alone in her bed as he'd been for years?

What if—and the look he was getting at this precise moment suggested it could be a reality—she was as attracted to him as he was to her? Mitch knew the answer to that. It was a very simple two-word answer. Or was it a question?

Why *not*?

CHAPTER THREE

DESPITE THE TENSION that always went with an assessment scenario, being closely watched and graded by both Jenna and a consultant trauma surgeon she had invited to help sign off the latest recruits to the FRAME network, one of her students was noticeably more relaxed than he had been at the beginning.

Andrew Mitchell was flying past every tick box on the assessment sheets. He had competently assessed the imaginary scenario for safety issues, cited the ways he would manage or mitigate risks, discounted the need to instigate a major incident plan and was moving through his patient assessment. A mannequin lay on the floor beneath a picture of a badly mangled motorbike and Mitch was up to assessing respiratory effort.

'Do I have any signs of respiratory distress?'

'Yes. Your patient has a respiration rate of greater than thirty. He's complaining of chest pain but is unable to speak in sentences. Heart rate is one hundred and thirty. Pulse oximetry is less than ninety percent and you've just lost a palpable radial pulse.'

'Do I see a jugular vein distension?'

'No.'

'Tracheal deviation?'

'Possible shift to the right.'

Mitch put the disc of the stethoscope onto one side of the chest. 'Breath sounds inaudible on the left.

'I'm diagnosing a tension pneumothorax,' he said moments later.

'Treatment?'

'A needle thoracostomy.'

'Talk me through the steps.'

Mitch easily listed the steps for a procedure that Jenna doubted he would have had reason to use during his time as a general practitioner. It sounded as if he'd done one only yesterday, however, and his manner was calm and confident.

'The recommended insertion site is the second intercostal space in the mid-clavicular line but, actually, insertion of the needle virtually anywhere in the correct haemotho-

rax will decompress a tension pneumothorax and if my patient's getting hypotensive
enough for the radial pulse to have disappeared then that puts his systolic blood pressure at less than eighty and makes this a
genuine emergency.'

The trauma surgeon exchanged a glance
with Jenna and the slight quirk of his eyebrow told her how impressed he was. It
was a bit absurd to feel this proud of Mitch
but—right from the opening minutes of this
course—there had been something about
this man that had captured her. She'd recognised that he was the first person since
Stefan that had triggered the kind of attraction she'd never expected—or wanted?—to
feel again but what had been even more of
a worry was how intimate that whispered
conversation had seemed yesterday while
he'd been having a go with the video laryngoscope.

'The needle needs to slide in over the
upper edge of the rib to avoid damage to
the neurovascular bundle on the lower edge
of each rib,' Mitch continued.

He was moving his hands as if he was actually performing the procedure as he was
explaining the steps. It was just as well she

was assessing him, Jenna thought, because it gave her a valid reason to be unable—or unwilling—to look away.

That sensation of intimacy had stayed with her last night and had only become stronger as she'd lain awake far longer than usual.

Jenna was, quite genuinely, not in the market for any kind of relationship. She'd meant what she'd said to people this morning that she wasn't about to let anything—or anyone—interfere with her commitment to the career she loved. What she hadn't bargained for, though, were the echoes of something that could only be shared by a couple who were completely in tune with each other. A particular look. A touch. The feeling of simply being held...

There was a part of her that still wanted that. So much that not having it in her life was a grief all of its own but she'd never considered trying to find it in isolation. Finding someone who wanted to hold her and touch her but nothing more than that. Maybe she was old-fashioned and hadn't approved of things like having a one-night stand or, good grief, what was that term she'd heard someone use recently—a sex buddy?

No…that notion was still enough to make her shudder but a one-off experience? With someone as attractive as Mitch? That might ease the ache of what had been missing in her life for a considerable period of time. Or it might, at least, allow her to gauge how great the effect of the total absence of physical connection with another person might be actually having on her.

Mitch would be perfect. If he was single, of course. If he was attracted to *her*.

There'd been moments in the last couple of days when she'd imagined that he was attracted to her. Like when she'd invited him to the front of the class to demonstrate the modified jaw thrust and he'd given her that almost smile when she'd praised him. And what about earlier today, when he'd been the one to answer the trickiest medical term she'd been able to come up with in relation to eye injuries?

Oh, yeah…she'd definitely seen something in his eyes that suggested this attraction was not one-sided.

So what was she going to do about it, if anything?

What would she do if she discovered he

was up for something a little more personal than being in a classroom together?

What if…?

Mitch was still speaking. Still sounding— and looking—remarkably relaxed. That curious intensity that she'd been aware of when she'd first met him had dissipated noticeably. As if he'd found whatever that important thing was that he'd been searching for. Was it crazy to feel a kind of connection here that suggested that Jenna *had* been the person who'd helped him find it?

'The signs and symptoms of a cardiac tamponade can certainly mimic a tension pneumothorax,' Mitch was saying. 'You can have the same hypotension, jugular vein distension and respiratory distress but the unilateral absence of breath sounds isn't present and…'

Oh, man… It was just as well that Jenna already knew Mitch was going to pass this assessment with no problems at all because she was barely listening as he talked to her colleague about differentiating between two critical situations that needed very different treatment.

All she could think about as she listened to his voice and tried to keep her gaze on his face instead of watching those expressive hands, wondering what it might be like to be touched by them, was the answer to that 'what if' question she didn't quite dare to articulate.

The answer was pretty simple, however. Why *not*?

She drank beer.

A boutique lager that came in a pretty, small bottle but it was still beer and not a glass of chardonnay or sauvignon blanc or maybe even an obscure cocktail that you might expect a sophisticated, intelligent young woman to choose when she was at the pub for a quick drink after work.

Mitch wasn't a bit surprised, mind you. It was just different, like everything else about Jenna Armstrong.

'I'll have what she's having,' he told the barman and, even if the beer wasn't going to be to his taste, it had been worth saying that just to catch the surprised delight in Jenna's eyes as he used a famous movie line that she clearly recognised. He also got the impression that, while she might not have expected him to watch rom coms any more than he'd expected her to drink beer, she rather liked this new piece of information about him.

Susie hadn't come to this planned gathering to celebrate the end of the intensive course and their collective success in making the grade to become FRAME practitioners. She'd apologised as she explained that her husband had a long shift that day and the nanny had her own commitments. She said that she hoped to catch up with everybody next year, when they would be due to come back for a refresher course but she looked disappointed at having to rush off.

She'd been shaking her head as she'd left with her certificate and new first aid kit. *'How did life suddenly get quite so complicated?'* she'd asked.

Mitch took a second sip of the boutique lager, which wasn't bad at all, and the baskets of deep-fried bar snacks that were arriving on the long wooden table, like tiny samosas and spring rolls, potato skins and battered scampi, looked delicious. Thank goodness he'd already warned his father that this social conclusion to the course was planned and that he might be a lot later home this evening. Ollie hadn't been bothered at all. Apparently a bubble bath was on the agenda as a treat and Grandpa was going to get *his* goodnight kiss as a bonus.

Mitch could relax and do something he hadn't done in a very long time, which was to simply enjoy the company of like-minded colleagues. Including Jenna. He wasn't a student any longer and she wasn't his instructor, which was making a surprising difference to how things felt between them.

Or perhaps that had something to do with the fact that Jenna had changed out of her uniform before coming to the pub. She was in denim jeans, white sneakers on her feet and a well-worn-looking leather jacket over a T-shirt. Her black curls had been ruffled by gusts of wind as they'd all walked to the nearest pub and it looked as though she'd used a bit of make-up despite being so quick to get changed after the course had formally concluded. Whatever the reason, Mitch was again wondering how on earth he had thought she wouldn't stand out in a crowd.

She was stunning.

And it was just as well he was sitting right beside her at this end of the long table because, otherwise, everybody would have noticed him staring at Jenna.

Or maybe not. All his fellow course attendees seemed to be involved in animated conversations. Peter and Jack at the other end of the table were talking about something that needed diagrams or possibly a flow chart to be drawn on a paper napkin. Melanie and Indira were listening to a story Ravi was telling them and, at this end of the table, Judith was frowning as she read a text message on her phone.

'Excuse me,' she said. 'It's my daughter. She had an antenatal check-up today so I'd better go and make a call somewhere a bit quieter and find out what's going on.' She squeezed out past Jenna, who moved sideways to make it easier which brought her close enough to Mitch for their thighs to touch.

It was impossible not to notice that Jenna didn't instantly move back but that was possibly because she hadn't noticed with other things that were happening, like Judith excusing herself and someone passing a basket to their end of the table.

'You guys had better get something to eat before it's all gone.'

Jenna beamed. 'Yay. I love potato skins. Especially when they're all crispy with Parmesan cheese on the top like this.' She bit into one of the snacks and Mitch had to deliberately turn away so he didn't keep watching her eat. That could well come across as being creepy, couldn't it?

'Looks like there are lots of good places to eat around here,' he said. 'Did you say you live not far away?'

'Just round the corner.' Jenna nodded. 'And you're right. I've got restaurants for just about every cuisine in the world within walking distance for take-outs. Afghani is my latest favourite.'

'Not something we've got in Allensbury,' Mitch said. 'Or not that I'm aware of, anyway.'

'You're not into take-outs?'

Mitch was taking another sip of his lager. This was a perfect opportunity to tell Jenna something about himself. That eating food that wasn't home cooked was quite a rare treat in the Mitchell household, because he was trying to keep his four-year-old son's diet as healthy as possible. He could also say that his dad was pretty conservative when it came to ethnic food but that would inevitably lead to talking about why three generations of Mitchell men were living in the same house and that would include his tragic personal history, which just wasn't appropriate in this time and space.

Being here, with this group—with Jenna—was not a part of his normal life. It was a treat. Like a take-out meal. Why spoil the enjoyment by talking about something that wasn't relevant, like why he was a single father? Especially when that information could very well change the vibe between himself and Jenna. It would undoubtedly make her move to put more distance between them and, he had to admit, if he could, he wanted to enjoy that frisson of physical touch—and the evidence of attraction that went with it—for a bit longer.

Judith came back but only to collect her bag and coat. 'Have to go,' she said. 'Everything's okay but my daughter sounds a bit stressed out. Thanks again, Jenna. The course was brilliant.'

Peter stood up as well. 'Better hit the road,' he sighed. 'Or I might be tempted to have another drink and it would be a long walk or a very expensive taxi ride home.' He shook Jack's hand. 'Nice to meet you. Let's stay in touch.'

'I'll walk out with you.' Jack smiled at Jenna. 'Thank you so much. I reckon we were pretty lucky to get you as our instructor.'

'I'll be in touch, too,' Jenna promised. 'I check in with all our FRAME practitioners on a regular basis.'

'Good to know,' Mitch murmured.

Maybe Jenna had heard his comment given the way her gaze flicked sideways. And maybe that was the reason that Mitch was aware of the sudden electricity in the air between them. That simmering attraction had ignited in some fashion, enough to make even the air sizzle.

Melanie was the last to leave, apart from Mitch. She also thanked Jenna profusely for her coaching.

'I wouldn't have got through that assessment scenario without you, either,' she added. 'I've always hated any kind of exam.'

'You did well. I don't think many people like performing in front of an audience but, you know, you'll find that's part of being a first responder in an emergency situation. Sometimes there's a crowd of onlookers and distressed family members but you *do* get used to it.'

Melanie made a face. 'If only I didn't live so far away. I'd love to take you up on that offer of getting more experience by going out on the road for an ambulance shift.'

'Talk to your local station. You'll find they will be very supportive of any FRAME doctors and they'll make space for you to join a crew. If you run into any problems, call me and I'll talk to the station manager. You're part of our team now.'

Mitch turned to Jenna before Melanie had reached the door of the pub. 'I didn't hear about that offer.'

'It was just chatting over lunch,' Jenna responded. 'But it applies to you as well. It's a great way to keep your skills up and get used to being ready for anything. I love the shifts I do.'

'I'm not sure where my closest ambulance station would be. We don't often have to call them in to transport patients from our medical centre. I think the last one came from Guildford. Or possibly from around here, given that Croydon is our other closest hospital. I could make enquiries about picking up the odd shift in an ED, I guess. That's where I used to work before switching to general practice.'

'Yes, you said you used to work in emergency.' Jenna nodded. 'It's a good idea. Or you could come here to do a few shifts. Sometimes it's very different working out in the field—as you know.' Jenna was sticking crumbs from the bottom of the potato skin basket to her finger as she spoke so she wasn't looking directly at Mitch but then she glanced up and caught his gaze. 'You could come out with me,' she added. 'In the rapid response vehicle. You get all the excitement of being sent to every potentially critical job and plenty of opportunity to use all your skills in situations that can be more challenging than an emergency department. Plus, you skip the downtime of having to transport patients to hospital or wait your turn for a Code Blue call if you're out on an ambulance.'

'Seriously?' Mitch was holding her gaze and he could actually feel his heart rate pick up at the prospect. 'You're allowed to take someone with you as an APP?'

'I'm the boss of my vehicle. I get to make the rules.' Jenna's grin was just a brief flash as she looked away, noticed the crumbs still stuck to her finger and put them in her mouth. 'Mmm.' She picked up the basket and shook it to see if she could find any more.

Meanwhile, Mitch was letting that idea roll around in his head and it was getting more exciting by the moment. It was like stepping back in time, even, to a point in his career when he had been exactly where he'd dreamed of being—the head of an emergency department that could erupt into the kind of chaos that came when back-to-back life-or-death emergencies had to be dealt with. A passion that he'd thought he'd never be able to recapture. A way of life that, at one point—before he'd met Tegan—had been his entire *raison d'être*.

'Could you do that?' Jenna asked. 'Or do you have commitments at home that might make it tricky?'

Was she asking him if he was single? *Available?*

Oh…wow…

He might have been justified in dismissing an opportunity to tell her about his private life earlier this evening but the answer to this specific query about his home commitments could change everything and Mitch didn't want that to happen. Amidst his gathering of those tendrils of a forgotten excitement his career was capable of providing, Jenna caught his gaze again and Mitch was instantly aware of another almost forgotten, but equally seductive sensation. This was far more powerful than an unexpected physical attraction to someone. This had all the sharpness and depth of an urgent level of desire.

He wanted this.

He wanted to recapture a snatch of the career he'd once loved so much.

And more than that, he wanted to ease an ache in his life that he had been ignoring for years.

Jenna didn't want a husband or a relationship that would interfere with her freedom to pursue a career she loved more than anything. She certainly wasn't interested in children. And…she was asking him if he wanted to spend more time with her. Professionally and…possibly personally?

There was only one way to find out but Mitch had to clear his throat before he could speak and, even then, his voice was a little hoarse.

'I'm single,' he told her. 'I could make it work. It wouldn't be a problem.'

He might not be telling her the whole truth but it wasn't a lie. Ollie was perfectly happy to be cared for by his grandpa and he would be totally protected from whatever came from Mitch spending more time with Jenna because there was no connection. Nobody in Allensbury, including his father, would need to know anything about what happened here, unless he chose to tell them. They would all support his interest in his new clinical responsibilities as a FRAME doctor and Mitch had at least two days a week when he wasn't rostered on at the medical centre so it would be easy to make himself available. He wanted to make himself available.

Mitch found a slow smile curving his lips after he'd spoken. The ball was back in Jenna Armstrong's court now. He was certainly available for a casual, professional kind of relationship. He could also be available for… what could he call that? Fringe benefits?

There was definitely a dreamlike quality to what was happening here. What had been happening for the last forty-eight hours, in fact—as if it had been scripted for a movie or something. Jenna felt like she was playing a part. That what was happening between herself and Mitch was meant to be…

He'd been a last-minute addition to that FRAME course and he'd captured her interest from the very beginning. That she was actually physically attracted to him had come as enough of a shock that if Jenna had simply met Mitch in passing, she would most likely have just kept moving. The fact that it would have been unacceptable if not unethical to explore an attraction while they were in a classroom situation with her as the instructor made it both impossible to escape and easy to deal with.

And because they had been forced to be together for those two days, they'd had opportunities to connect and that attraction had become more familiar. Less scary. Welcome, even?

That hadn't been the reason that Jenna had invited Mitch to do some shifts with her in the rapid response vehicle, however. She genuinely liked him and was equally impressed with the clinical skills and intelligence he clearly had. He'd been an emergency department doctor in the past so it was highly likely she could learn as much from him as he might from being out on the road with her.

Jenna had to admit that the attraction might explain why she'd suggested he walked home with her, mind you, under the pretext of making a copy of the printout of her coming roster so that he could take it home and choose a date for his first shift with her. Not that she was about to try and seduce him or anything. She just wanted to be in his company a little longer. To be honest, though, there was something rather intimate about leading him up the narrow staircase that led to her attic flat a few blocks away from the pub they'd left.

''Scuse the mess,' she said, as she opened her front door. 'I've been packing and sorting the paperwork for a longer course I'm heading off to tomorrow up in Manchester. When we work with nurses or paramedics to bring them up to speed with FRAME skill set requirements, we do a five-day initiation course.'

It felt like she was prattling, which she probably was. Because Jenna was suddenly nervous. She hadn't felt like this in so long, it was like time-travelling back to being an awkward teenager. She hadn't even invited a man back into this small flat and it seemed to have shrunk considerably in the last few seconds. It felt stuffy, too, as if there wasn't enough air. Maybe she should open a window?

'There's a beer in the fridge if you fancy

it. I'll just find that file and warm up the printer.'

'No, thanks. Not when I'll be driving soon.'

Did he want to escape as soon as possible? Had she been reading signals incorrectly? Like when he hadn't moved his leg when she'd shifted on that seat in the pub and her thigh had come into contact with his? The thought prompted a curious glance in Mitch's direction. That touch might have felt weirdly hot on her skin, despite the layers of clothing between them, but maybe he hadn't even noticed it?

But he was smiling at her. 'A coffee would be great, though,' he said. 'Shall I put the jug on?'

Such an ordinary sort of thing to say. And it had the effect of taking all the awkwardness out of him being here. Even when Jenna joined him in the tiny kitchen to find the instant coffee and some mugs and they were so close together that Mitch's arm brushed her back as he reached to open the fridge to get the milk, it still felt okay.

More than okay...

Jenna wasn't sure if she leaned into the touch of that arm or whether it had been Mitch's choice to abandon opening the fridge and let his arm curl more closely around her body but it didn't seem to matter because, as she looked up, she found Mitch looking down at her and the expression in his eyes took her breath away.

How could she have thought for a moment that he hadn't been aware of that touch of their thighs earlier this evening? The strength of the desire she could see in his eyes was enough to create a shaft of sensation deep in her belly that felt like fireworks going off. She had completely forgotten— probably deliberately—what even an echo of that kind of desire could feel like. The reminder was enough to make her lips feel suddenly dry and she couldn't stop herself moistening them with the tip of her tongue.

Mitch watched her do that but he said nothing. The only sound in this cramped space was the bubble of water coming to the boil in the electric jug and then it shut itself off automatically with a dull click but they were still staring at each other, as if they were both caught. Wondering how or where they could find shelter from the force of what was happening here, perhaps?

It was Jenna who finally moved. Who came up on tiptoe but she wouldn't have been able to reach Mitch's lips to kiss him if he hadn't bent his head.

It wasn't a real kiss. Jenna just felt an overwhelming need to know what it would be like to touch a man's lips with her own for the first time in for ever. She even kept her eyes open as that touch happened. A touch that was so soft it was kind of like hearing the faint notes of a favourite song wafting from an open window nearby but so nice that she moved her head a little to one side and then the other, a stroking movement intended to capture a bit more of that feeling.

Pulling back, Jenna saw that Mitch had *his* eyes open as well and once again they were staring at each other. And it felt as if they were communicating by sharing nothing but ripples of emotion.

Astonishment.

Delight.

A longing for more…a lot more.

But, even with the strength of those emotions, the next touch of their lips was still gentle, although nowhere near as soft as the first time. The real difference was that they both closed their eyes. And that it morphed into a very real kiss in a matter of moments. When Mitch's hands shaped Jenna's body, however, softly cupping her breast as his thumb stroked over her hidden nipple, she sensed the same kind of wonder that she'd felt about kissing him—as if this was something new in his life again as well.

Something changed at that point. Maybe because Jenna could feel a connection that was very different to this physical desire. Was she projecting her own mixed feelings that she needed this so much but it felt almost as if she was dismissing a very important part of her past? It didn't feel wrong, though. Instead, it bestowed something positive on this. Something caring. Or at least something that, for Jenna, made it more acceptable than a casual encounter that had no significance.

Exchanging emotions wasn't enough as their gazes met this time.

'I…um… I'm a bit out of practice with this kind of thing.' Jenna's voice was husky. 'Actually, *very* out of practice.'

'You and me both.' The muscles in Mitch's throat moved as he swallowed. 'It's been… good grief…years.'

So she'd been right. This was as new again for him as it was for her. The reasons why didn't matter. Jenna remembered that odd feeling that he'd seen her as the person who could give him something he'd been searching for.

Now maybe she knew what that something was. And it was something that was also missing from her own life.

'It's because I haven't been looking for a relationship,' she said quietly. 'It's still not something I want.'

'Neither do I.'

'It makes it difficult, doesn't it? To...you know...find, um...company.'

'Mmm...'

He was watching her carefully. Waiting for what she was about to say.

But there was something else she thought she could see in his eyes. Hope...?

'Skills get rusty,' she murmured, 'if they don't get used every once in a while.'

'I've heard that.' Mitch closed his eyes as he whispered the words, his breath coming out in a slow sigh.

It was Jenna's turn to swallow carefully. 'Even if they are a bit rusty—' she needed to catch another breath '—it's possible to fix that. If...you know...you want to.'

Mitch's eyes were open again. His gaze was fixed on Jenna's with all the intensity they had been a few minutes ago before that first, butterfly wing kiss.

'Oh… I want to,' he said softly. 'But what about you?'

Again, Jenna stood on tiptoe and, this time, she reached up to put her hands on Mitch's cheeks to encourage him to bend his head so that she could kiss him.

She only had time for a single word before his mouth covered hers. Before she felt him lift her into his arms and knew he was about to carry her to her bed.

'Same…'

CHAPTER FOUR

EQUIPMENT IN THE back of the rapid response vehicle bounced and clattered as the vehicle crossed the central island in the road, aiming for a gap amongst oncoming traffic. Cars and trucks were doing their best to pull aside and make room for the emergency vehicle with its flashing lights and siren going. A warning blast on the airhorn was enough to make a pedestrian change his mind fast about the wisdom of ducking in front of them to weave through the rush-hour congestion.

Mitch was in the front passenger seat. Jenna was driving. She bounced them back over the raised concrete edges of the island as they cleared the intersection, flashing him a quick grin as she noticed him reach for the handle above the door to steady himself so he didn't lurch sideways.

'All good?'

'Couldn't be better.' He looked at the satellite navigation screen built into the dashboard. 'We're getting close.'

Jenna was accelerating as she overtook vehicles pulling to the side ahead of them. The heads of a line of people at a bus stop turned in unison to watch them go past and Mitch could imagine that there was a collective bubble above their heads asking, 'What's happened? How bad is it?'

Maybe Jenna had seen that as well in her peripheral vision. 'Any more details coming through?'

'Paramedics on scene say they're dealing with a collapsed lung. Respiration rate currently sixty and oxygen saturation levels are under eighty.'

A single nod from Jenna showed that she had taken the information on board but her focus was on getting them to the scene as back-up as quickly as possible had just ramped up. She had to brake hard enough to be sure that cars were all stopping to let them go through a red traffic light safely and then she put her foot down again. Mitch was still hanging onto the handle, to stop him tipping too far towards her, as they rounded a sharp corner.

It was a hit and run they were heading to. The sixth and possibly final job on the first shift that Mitch had come to spend with Jenna. An older pedestrian that had been clipped by a van and it sounded like he wasn't doing too well at all. A collapsed lung could be caused by a pneumothorax, with air collecting outside the lung and inside the chest wall, probably due to damage from a broken rib. It could be a haemopneumothorax with a mix of blood and air or a tension pneumothorax, like the scenario that had been used for his FRAME practitioner assessment a couple of weeks ago.

Whatever the cause, this time Mitch would get to do the treatment for real because getting precisely this kind of experience was why he had taken up Jenna's offer to join her on some of her APP single responder shifts. And, this time, someone's life could very well depend on it.

Mitch took a deep breath as they rounded another curve and could see flashing lights and a solid wall of traffic ahead of them. A police officer waved them towards the side of the road and Jenna moved forward slowly now, with one set of wheels on the footpath as bystanders got out of the way. Mitch was totally focused. Ready for anything. Exhilarated, in fact. He hadn't felt this *alive*, he realised, for a very, very long time.

In a way, it reminded him of when he'd been a kid, about Ollie's age or a bit older, and it was Christmas Eve and excitement was building to an almost unbearable level because he knew something big was about to happen but he had no idea what it might be. What he did know was that taking up Jenna's offer to join her on the road was the best decision he could have made because it had brought an entirely new dimension into his life.

As had that single night with the woman who was driving this vehicle like an absolute pro. Not that he was about to let a single, mind-blowing detail of that extraordinary taste of a previous life derail his concentration right now but he was still feeling relieved that their first meeting today since that evening hadn't been awkward. Okay, he knew they were both thinking about what had happened in Jenna's flat—in her bed—but it had been pushed aside as something irrelevant to their professional time together today. It was only important because it had given them a connection that added a level of friendship, or maybe trust, to their imminent working relationship.

No. It was important for something even more significant than what was happening now. It was linked to the past because it had also been a catalyst for a major change in his life. Deep down, he knew that that night together was a part of this new dimension. A reawakening of the man he'd once been. Before life had derailed *him*.

'You get to run this job,' Jenna told him, as she pulled the vehicle to a halt near an ambulance that had its back doors open to reveal uniformed paramedics crouched over a figure on the stretcher. 'Pretend it's a FRAME call-out. I'll only step in if you ask me to. Or if I think it's in the patient's best interests.' She caught his gaze, pausing for a heartbeat before opening her door. 'All good?'

It was the same question she'd asked before, when the speed of their vehicle had had them lurching around. And that hadn't been the first time, either. A tiny blip at the back of his brain reminded Mitch that she'd asked it that night, as well—after the most incredible sex he'd ever experienced. It was almost like a private code between them already and what was becoming a practised response was right on the tip of his tongue.

'Couldn't be better.'

One of the paramedics on scene at the hit and run knew Jenna but he could see that she was staying behind her extra crew member and that the stranger was wearing a high-vis jacket with 'DOCTOR' emblazoned on the back so that made him the highest medical authority here.

Not that Mitch needed a label to enable him to take control. He had an aura of confidence and skill that made it automatic and Jenna found herself admiring the calm way he was gathering as much information as he could in the shortest possible time from what he could see and hear around him and the questions he was asking the paramedics who had been treating the patient for his chest trauma including broken ribs and possible internal injuries.

Sixty-four-year-old Gerald was still conscious, despite falling blood pressure and having difficulty breathing.

'I'm Mitch,' He crouched at the head of the stretcher after the rapid-fire information-sharing. 'I've got Jenna with me as well and we're going to help look after you and get you safely into hospital just as quickly as we can.'

'Okay…thanks…' Gerald's voice was muffled by his panting breaths beneath the oxygen mask.

Mitch glanced up. 'Blood pressure now?'

'Systolic still dropping. Eighty-four.'

'Oxygen saturation?'

'Seventy-eight.'

'Has he got a pelvic wrap on?'

'Yes.'

'We need another line in. Preferably central. Jenna? Could you pass me the portable ultrasound, please? And set up for the line?'

'Sure.'

It was getting crowded in the back of this ambulance as its crew shifted back to make room for the more advanced procedures their back-up medics could provide. Gerald already had a peripheral IV line in his arm but a central line was an intravenous catheter placed in a large vein near the heart and it had the advantage of letting them infuse a large volume of fluid rapidly, which their patient might well need if his blood pressure fell any further and he crashed.

Jenna could see Mitch using the probe

from the ultrasound as she set out the cannula and attachments, adhesive coverings and alcohol wipes she needed to insert the subclavian line. She could sense his concentration and how fast his brain was working, not only to interpret the grainy images of what he was seeing on the screen but to weigh up every treatment option and the order they might need to be done to keep this critically ill person alive.

'Okay,' he said moments later. 'Here's the plan.' He was speaking to the medical team around him but including Gerald as well. 'You've got a collapsed lung and it's getting harder for you to breathe, so we're going to give you some more pain medication and try putting a needle into your chest. If that doesn't help enough, we're going to give you some stronger medication that will make you very sleepy. You won't know what's happening but we'll be taking over helping you to breathe for a while—until we can get you into hospital.'

Gerald nodded. He seemed to be trying to say something but his words were no more than incoherent gasps and his anxious head movements gradually slowed as the medication took effect.

Jenna had the central line in place by the time Mitch had the chest decompression needle inserted but the numbers on the monitor weren't going in the right direction.

'O2 sats down to seventy-four.' Jenna knew they were going to have to do something a lot more invasive and they probably only had one shot to obtain control of the airway and to improve how much oxygen was circulating. She'd have to step in if Mitch didn't move fast but he was speaking even before she'd finished her sentence. He'd also seen the numbers on the monitor.

'Let's have the RSI kit,' he said. 'We're going to do a crash intubation and see if we can get those sats up. I need one person to pre-oxygenate. Jenna, could you draw up the ketamine and suxamethonium, please? And I need a rolled-up towel to go under his shoulders.'

It was the first time Jenna had seen Mitch work on a real person rather than a mannequin but it was no surprise that his intubation technique was smooth and confident. It was also successful but even with the high level of oxygen being provided, the figure on the monitor remained dangerously low.

Mitch caught Jenna's gaze. They were

going to lose this patient if they didn't try something else. She waited a beat to see if the procedure she was thinking of was also at the top of Mitch's list. A surgical intervention only authorised to be performed out of hospital by doctors or paramedics with advanced training.

'Finger thoracostomy?' he suggested quietly.

'It's what I'd do.' Jenna nodded.

Gerald was unconscious. Unaware of the slice of the scalpel or the pressure of Mitch's gloved finger pushing through the muscle of his chest wall. The white towel underneath that side of the chest caught the rush of blood that obviously had air pressure behind it but the bleeding subsided relatively quickly. As quickly as the percentage of oxygen in the blood being displayed on the monitor began to increase. Back into the eighties. Into the nineties when Jenna could see Mitch releasing a relieved breath of his own but then he turned instantly to the next issue.

'Blood pressure's still too low,' he said. 'Let's get more fluids up and I think it's time to move. He could well be bleeding somewhere else. Jenna?'

'Totally agree.' She nodded. 'We'll stay

with him in the ambulance. Can one of you guys follow us in with our vehicle, please?'

'I could do that.' A policewoman was standing at the open back door. 'I need to come in with you, anyway. I've got a little girl here who says that your patient is her grandfather. We're trying to contact other members of her family but it will be easier to meet them at the hospital.'

Jenna blinked. Was that what Gerald had been trying to tell them when he was so anxious before they knocked him out to take over his breathing? The policewoman moved and now Jenna could see a girl who was about five or six years old. Her long dark braids were framing a very pale, frightened little face and the child was crying silently, fat tears rolling down her cheeks.

'Oh…sweetheart…' Jenna stopped packing up some of their gear in preparation for transport and stepped towards the doors. She jumped out and crouched down so that she was on the same level as the girl. 'I know it's scary,' she said, 'but Dr Mitch is looking after your grandad and we're going to take him to the hospital where there are even more doctors to take good care of him.' She reached out to brush the tears from that small face. 'What's your name?'

'K-Kirsty.'

'Can you be brave, Kirsty? And come to the hospital with...' She glanced up at the policewoman.

'Lydia,' she supplied.

Kirsty nodded slowly.

'Good girl...'

Jenna only intended to smile at Kirsty but somehow she ended up with two small arms around her neck and legs that wound themselves around her waist as she stood up. For just a heartbeat, and then another, she pressed her cheek against that soft hair, closing her eyes as she felt and responded to that plea for comfort. When she opened her eyes again, she could see over Kirsty's shoulder into the back of the ambulance where things were moving fast to tidy up the clutter of used packaging and equipment enough to make sure they could monitor their patient and keep anything they might need for the journey close at hand.

Mitch was already seated at the head of the stretcher, holding and squeezing the bag mask to keep Gerald breathing. He had the monitor screen close by but, right now, he was watching Jenna and Kirsty and there was a concerned frown on his face. Because she was holding them up? Fair enough.

'Come on,' she said, gently disengaging the limbs of the frightened child. 'I'm going to put you in my special car because Lydia's going to drive you to the hospital. I've got to go and help take care of your grandad.'

If Mitch had shown his ability to take command of a tense medical situation when they'd arrived on scene, he was even more in his element as they rushed the stretcher into the Trauma Resus room at the hospital they transported Gerald to. The specialist ED consultant leading the trauma team took a second look as someone led the transfer of their patient from stretcher to bed.

'On my count. On three. One…two… *three…*'

There was controlled chaos behind them as everybody played their part in rearranging the attachments for an oxygen supply, replacing ambulance monitoring gear with their own, hooking up a mechanical ventilator and taking a new set of vital signs. Someone was also cutting away the remnants of Gerald's clothing to expose his entire body for a detailed examination. It would be a few moments before everybody was ready for a detailed handover.

'Mitch?' The consultant took a third glance. 'What on earth are you doing out on the road? Last I heard you were HOD at St Barnabas.'

Jenna's head turned sharply. Mitch had told her that he'd worked in an emergency department before moving into general practice but he'd been Head of Department? In one of London's most prestigious trauma centres?

No wonder he had that kind of confidence she'd seen on scene today.

But why on earth had he gone from one end of the spectrum to the other as far as fast-paced medical careers could be lined up?

Mitch was simply shaking his head, dismissing the query. His attention was on the consultant in charge of the airway and breathing who was examining the hole in the side of Gerald's chest.

'Can you feel the lung? Has it re-inflated?'

'Yes. And we'll get a tube in to make sure it stays that way. Good job sorting that in the field. What was the initial blood loss?'

'Only a couple of hundred mils. Not

enough to account for that level of hypotension.'

Jenna stepped back as the lead ambulance paramedic detailed their findings on arrival at the scene and Mitch took over to cover the more advanced interventions they'd supplied. There was ultrasound gear being manoeuvred into position beside the bed, a radiographer was getting ready to take any X-rays ordered and so many other people around that she could only catch a glimpse of Gerald.

Near the half-open door to this highly specialised and equipped space, she could see into the emergency department and the central desk. Lydia, the policewoman, was standing there and she was holding Kirsty's hand. A nurse was leading a distressed-looking woman towards the pair. Kirsty's mother? Gerald's daughter? Jenna felt a lump in her throat that was actually painful as she saw the expression on the woman's face.

She knew that kind of fear.

The kind of despair that could come later as a family was shattered.

She watched the woman scoop Kirsty into her arms and remembered the feeling of having those small limbs wound around her and that made the lump even bigger. Sharper. Enough to make it hard to breathe so Jenna automatically turned away. She watched what was happening in Resus for another minute but then moved out of the way completely. She could wait in the car until Mitch came out and make herself useful by seeing what needed to be restocked with their gear and starting on their own paperwork, which would be added to the ambulance report forms.

Finding a smile for Kirsty as she walked past, Jenna sincerely hoped that the news this family would be receiving later on would be good. Or at least hopeful. It was satisfying to know that everything possible that could have been done medically to make that a possibility had been done at the scene.

And done brilliantly. Jenna would have no hesitation at all in letting Mitch lead any job she was dispatched to when he was with her. She would trust him with her own life with any medical emergency.

She had already trusted him with her body in another way, after all.

Phew... It was just as well she was already walking through the automatic doors to leave the emergency department as that thought entered her mind because it immediately triggered memories of that night that actually felt like Mitch was touching her again. She could feel the intensity of the strokes of his hands. The touch of his fingers. The glide of his tongue. She was even aware of a spear of sensation deep inside to remind her of how *that* had felt as well and a ripple that was a faint echo of just how powerful her climax had been.

Oh, *my*… Jenna was grateful for the cool air outside, knowing that her cheeks had to have reddened. She knew they'd both been thinking about it when Mitch had arrived on station and they'd made eye contact for the first time since he'd left her flat that evening but that had been okay. There had been an instant, tacit agreement that it was not something they were going to think about, let alone discuss, while they were together in a professional arena. It had felt almost like friends thinking about a shared night out of going to the movies or out for dinner or something. It had only been intended to be a one-off, after all—to see how rusty they might both have become in the area of sexual skills?

Andrew Mitchell hadn't been at all rusty. She almost wished she hadn't reassured him about that at the time because, that way, they have come to an agreement to arrange another skill refresher session.

Any disturbing feeling of being disloyal to Stefan's memory had worn off since then so Jenna didn't even try and contradict the assessment that the sex with Mitch had been the best sex she'd ever experienced in her life. But how big a part of that was due to having gone without intimate touch for so long? A starving person would probably find any kind of food delicious, wouldn't they?

There was a level of curiosity in Jenna's mind now. Would a second time with Mitch be as good as the first? Because she was still thinking about that as Mitch climbed back into the passenger seat of the car, Jenna instantly found something else to talk about. Something professional.

'How good was that? You got to tick off three major skill sets that you haven't used for a while. Needle decompression, intubation *and* a finger thoracostomy as a bonus.' She was speaking a little too fast but Mitch was smiling.

'I think he's going to be okay. They're taking him up to Theatre. Ultrasound showed some abdominal bleeding that looks like it could be coming from a ruptured spleen. He's got blood products running now, which has stabilised his blood pressure.' His smile widened. 'It was a great job, wasn't it?'

Jenna nodded. 'And I have to say, I was impressed with how not rusty you were with your skills.'

Uh-oh…that was rather too similar to what she'd said to him that night. Jenna grabbed the handpiece to her radio from its clip on the dashboard. 'Rapid Response One available,' she told Control. 'We'll return to station to restock but we're still okay to respond in the meantime.'

Mitch clicked his seatbelt into place but he wasn't saying anything so Jenna filled the silence quickly.

'Not that I'm surprised you did so well,' she said. 'There I was thinking you'd done a registrar rotation or something in an ED but you were head of department? At St Barnabas?' Jenna couldn't help the admiration in her tone. 'Bit of a career change to become a GP, wasn't it?'

Mitch shrugged. 'Crossroads in your life appear for all sorts of reasons' was all he said.

Jenna turned out of the hospital entrance-way to join the heavy traffic of a late London weekday afternoon. She had to weave across lanes so it didn't feel like an awkward silence between them. She wasn't just thinking about what lane she needed to be in, however, because it was impossible not to pick up on the message that his dramatic change in career was not something that Mitch wanted to talk about.

Fair enough.

Would she want to talk about the how and why of how she'd ended up in this particular branch of her career as a paramedic?

Absolutely not. And, if he'd been nosey about her personal history when they'd first spent time together, she would have put distance between them as fast as possible and that night would never have happened. And she was very, very glad that it had happened. This connection she'd discovered with this man was very new.

It was exciting.

She'd taken a huge leap reintroducing sex back into her life again and that time with Mitch had confirmed that being close to someone like that was definitely a missing piece. Whether she could find anyone else that might be interested in an occasional, purely physical interaction was an entirely different matter, mind you. But…maybe she didn't need to…?

'Good to know that you thought my skills weren't too rusty.' Mitch was smiling at her again. 'But there's always room for improvement, isn't there? Practice makes perfect.'

Oh…man…

That *smile*…

That flash of complete understanding in her eyes. Jenna had been completely in sync with the skills he was actually talking about when he'd suggested that practice made perfect. Okay…when he'd pretty much asked if she was up for a repeat of their 'no strings', 'no pressure' sexual encounter from the other week.

Not that she'd responded straight away. No…another emergency call had been a great excuse to shelve saying anything and it wasn't until the shift had ended more than an hour later that she'd caught Mitch's gaze and suggested a debrief over a beer or coffee—at her flat—and the way she'd held his gaze had told him that she had understood his earlier, subtle invitation. And that she was more than happy to accept it.

She understood a lot of things without needing any kind of explanation, Mitch thought as he followed her up those narrow stairs again and waited for her to unlock the door to her flat. Like the way she'd known how hard it had been for him to watch that dramatisation of a nasty horse-riding accident. And that he didn't want to talk about the reasons he'd left his position at St Barnabas to become a small town GP.

He liked that she was respecting his privacy but it actually had a contradictory effect because Mitch found himself wanting to tell her the truth about why he'd given up the career he loved.

About Ollie...

Except that would change things and they were perfect just as they were. Mitch pushed the door shut behind him as Jenna dropped her keys onto a table and hung her uniform jacket over the back of a chair. She pulled pens from her shirt pocket and a tourniquet and notepad from a pocket in her trousers and then stooped to unzip the sides of her heavy boots.

It looked as though she was getting undressed already and Mitch could feel his heart rate pick up and the curl of desire in his belly grow instantly a hell of a lot more noticeable.

'Maybe I can help with that…' He walked closer to Jenna and reached for the button at the top of her shirt. 'I'm not feeling that confident in my button undoing skills. I think… maybe I need a bit of practice?'

He was watching her face as his fingers brushed her skin while fumbling with the small button. He saw the way she caught her bottom lip between her teeth but that didn't quite stop the delighted smile trying to break out. He felt the way she came up on tiptoe as that button popped free and dipping his head to respond to that invitation to kiss her was enough to drive any other thoughts from his head.

Almost…

Maybe he was trying to find justification for keeping his personal life so private because the thought that occurred to him in that split second before his lips covered hers was that people who respected the privacy of others often preferred to keep their own lives private and maybe that was a part of the trust that had made a connection with Jenna so easy.

Perhaps they knew enough about each

other as it was so he didn't need to feel that he was being dishonest in some way.

They'd both turned their backs on the possibility of significant relationships and there always a reason why people did that. A big reason, usually.

They'd chosen each other—or fate had done it for them—to step out of a sexual desert they'd been in for a long time and they'd discovered something amazing.

Mitch was kissing Jenna again now. And she was kissing him back. He could taste that deliciousness that had been haunting him ever since last time. He could feel her fingers on his belt—and the buckle—and the touch created an anticipation that was just as delicious. Until her fingers brushed lower as she undid the buckle and anticipation got blindsided by an irresistible need to get a whole lot closer.

It was way too tempting to stop thinking and give in to simply *feeling*…

He would tell her the truth at some point, of course he would.

But not now. Because it was totally irrelevant.

CHAPTER FIVE

THERE WERE A huge number of towns and cities that Jenna had been to during the years of establishing the FRAME network and she'd always loved the travelling—the disruption of a normal routine and the distraction of exploring new places.

Until now.

She wasn't loving being away from London this time, despite being in York, one of her favourite cities, and this being a five-day initiation course that provided enough time to really get to know an interesting group of mostly nurses who had come from small villages and remote communities to upskill in careers they were all passionate about. Not only that, she was also doing one of her favourite things in that she was training a trainer.

Rob was a skilled paramedic in his fifties, who'd been an APP like herself but had moved into teaching due to a bad back injury and, to his surprise, found he was loving his new direction. He was engaging, often funny and his students were responding in a way that told Jenna their new instructor was going to be one of their best. He'd been sitting in on her taking most of the sessions for the first couple of days but was gradually taking over. By Day Five and the assessments, he would be running this intake alone.

Right now, Rob was wrapping up a session that had never been a favourite for Jenna.

Paediatrics.

In the early days these sessions had, in fact, provided one of the biggest hurdles she'd had to overcome but also one of the biggest incentives to train people to the very best of their abilities in the hope that it could prevent another person having to go through what she'd endured.

The anatomical and physiological stuff was easy enough, covering the major differences from adults that influenced assessment and treatment, like the larger head and shorter necks, larger tongues and higher larynx, and normal ranges for vital signs like respiration and heart rates. The harder stuff was what Rob was teaching now and Jenna automatically found herself taking a mental step backwards. Distancing herself from the session's content enough to make it impersonal.

Trying to ignore that awareness like a soft drumbeat in the back of her head. Or was it in her heart?

'So, there you are.' Rob had a scene on the screen of a small, crumpled figure lying on a patch of grass. The background was blurred but you could see it was a child's playground. 'You're first on the scene and you've got an unresponsive kid. Before we get into how we're going to assess and treat this little guy, let's run over all the possible causes of paediatric collapse.'

It was just a single word, that drumbeat. A name that Jenna could hear again and again and again.

Eli... Eli... Eli...

Even now, as year after year had ticked past, it was still there. Nothing like as painful, of course, but she knew it was never going to disappear. She didn't want it to. Memories were precious. It wasn't something she was ever going to experience again but it was a part of her history. Her story. She had once been a wife. And a mother.

Rob was doing a great job eliciting the correct answers before revealing the next line of text on the screen. Under the heading of hypoxia, there were now bullet points of airway obstruction—with secondary headings of foreign body, croup, epiglottis and asthma—anaphylaxis, near drowning and cardiac causes that also needed a breakdown into areas like congenital heart disease, arrhythmias and heart failure.

'We're missing a couple, guys. Have a think.'

An older nurse spoke quietly. 'I went to a family in our village once. Their toddler had got himself all caught up in the strings for the venetian blind. He'd suffocated.'

Rob's nod was solemn. 'That's one of them, all right. Sadly not that uncommon, either.'

'Asphyxia' came up on the screen.

'There's another condition that is not uncommon in children. It can start at any age and someone with Down syndrome, metabolic disorders or autism may have this as well. Causes can include infection, brain injury, a tumour—'

'Epilepsy,' someone called. 'They're unresponsive due to a seizure.' The answer was accompanied by a headshake. 'I should have thought of that straight off. My nephew used to get them all the time. Seems to have grown out of them, though.

'And other kids have seizure activity that's very well controlled with medication. So when would you be more likely to get called in, do you think?'

'When the medication's not working. When the seizure doesn't stop.'

Rob gave the student a 'thumbs up' sign and then the last line of text appeared. Status epilepticus. And that was the point that Jenna let her focus drift completely, even turning her head enough to look out of the window. She could see a section of the ancient city walls that York was so famous for. She'd go and walk there again when classes were finished for the day. The sights were all familiar but she loved them. She might stop and have a coffee in the little shop in Barker's Tower and she'd never miss the highlight of Clifford's Tower, the largest remaining section of York castle.

But even the prospect of revisiting a place she enjoyed so much wasn't enough to squash the nagging feeling that she wanted to be somewhere else and Jenna knew exactly where it was she wanted to be. In Croydon. More specifically, in her own flat. Or out on the road. Because, even more specifically, she wanted to be with Mitch.

She was missing him.

She'd only known him a matter of weeks. They'd only been working together in the rapid response unit a handful of times and they'd been to bed together on even fewer occasions but his company had become an important part of her life.

Jenna really liked him.

Okay…she really, *really* liked him. She admired his professional skill and his impressive intelligence but there was a lot more to his company that she was appreciating more every time they were together. He had a compassion and gentleness with his patients that was completely genuine and he was, quite probably, the nicest man she'd ever met. Apart from Stefan, of course. But he wasn't so nice he was too good to be true. She'd seen him deal with unpleasant people in no uncertain terms and he still had that air of mystery about him that was intriguing. Why *had* he left such a prestigious position at St Barnabas?

She would have enjoyed Mitch's company—the satisfaction of working together and the stimulation of having a professional conversation—without the bonus of the sex but, if she was really honest, that was a huge part of this pull she was feeling to be back home. She knew that she'd been missing that physical closeness with another human being but she'd had no idea how much more than something purely physical it could be. Those times with Mitch could make the world stop turning for a while. Could make it impossible to have the head space to include anything from the past. Or the future. For as long as it lasted, that connection—that exquisite tension and pleasure—was all that existed. In nearly a decade, Jenna had never found anything else that came close to giving her even a temporary belief that life could be as perfect for her as for the luckiest people alive.

Rob was moving on, directing the class into exercises for assessing and treating paediatric emergencies and he was managing so well that Jenna knew she could excuse herself from the room for a few minutes.

Enough time to check her rosters for the coming week or two and see what days she might be back on the road in South London. And to send a text message to see if Mitch was available to share that time with her?

Yes… Even knowing when she was going to see him again would prevent that knot of tension from growing any more disruptive. What was it, exactly? A worry that this new dimension in her life might vanish as unexpectedly as it had arrived in her life? Maybe Jenna just needed to be more confident that this arrangement she had with Mitch was providing something they both wanted. That they both needed, even.

Just to be on the safe side, though, she would send that text. Holding her hand up to indicate a five-minute interval, she tilted her head to acknowledge Rob's smile and nod and slipped out of the classroom.

When his text came in response to hers, almost instantly, to say that he'd look forward to coming out on the road with her next Friday, Jenna found herself holding her phone against her heart, leaning back against the corridor wall and closing her eyes as she let her breath out in a sigh.

She felt like a teenager who'd just been

asked on a date by the boy she'd had a crush on for ever.

It felt a lot like she might be falling in love with Andrew Mitchell which was most definitely not supposed to be happening.

But what if it was?

A new thought occurred to Jenna and it seemed like her entire body wanted to consider it. What if Mitch felt the same way she did about not wanting children in his life? They wouldn't need to consider anything as formal as marriage or anything but it was quite possible to imagine their connection lasting…well…for ever…?

One look at the sky as Mitch headed towards London early on a Friday made him think that if he was sensible, he'd be staying at home on his day off. It was clearly going to be stormy and the forecast had warnings of possible thunder- or even hail-storms. He could have caught up on some shopping and housework and then had a fire going so that the house was lovely and warm for when Ollie got home from school but no… he was on his way to spend a day with Jenna and there would probably be a spate of the kind of road accidents that always came with bad weather. He remembered the chaos that could accumulate back in his days in the emergency department but he'd been working inside where it was nice and dry.

Today he'd be working outside and could be getting miserably cold and wet where it would be so much harder to do something like inserting an IV or splinting a fracture and...and he hadn't felt this happy in a very long time.

He'd found himself thinking about Jenna rather a lot between the times they spent together. Sometimes he'd remember how much he enjoyed a particular conversation with her or how impressive it was to watch her work. Other times, he could remember just an expression on her face, the way a brief glance had made him feel so good or...oh, *help*... the feel and taste of her skin in those secret places. Mitch had to blow out a slow breath as what was becoming a very familiar shaft of sensation came from nowhere and obliterated any other coherent thought.

Fortunately it only lasted for as long as it took to blink but the echoes were still astonishingly strong. He must have felt the same way with Tegan but it was so long ago he couldn't really remember. This—

with Jenna—felt completely new. Amazing enough to remind him of what it had been like to discover sex as a teenager. Important enough to create a hint of something that felt like nervousness because he didn't want it to stop anytime soon.

Anytime at all…?

The first spots of rain spattered his windscreen as Mitch merged with Greater London commuters. The red traffic lights ahead took so long to change from red to green that he could allow his thoughts to wander again. There was no real reason for this 'no strings' relationship with Jenna to end, was there? Not if Jenna was getting as much out of it as he was. Maybe…one day…he might even be able to introduce her to Ollie.

Mitch knew she might not want children to interfere with her career and that was fair enough, but he also knew that she was good with them—he'd seen the way she'd been with that little girl, Kirsty, the granddaughter of the man who'd been so badly injured in that hit and run. He'd been caught, not only by how easily he'd seen her win the trust of that frightened child but the way she'd looked with Kirsty in her arms. That moment when Jenna had given her a cuddle and the expression on her face when she'd looked up and caught his gaze.

It had only been for a heartbeat but, for that instant, Jenna had looked more vulnerable than he'd ever seen her. As if she'd been spotted doing something she didn't want anyone else to see. It hadn't been the first time that Mitch had wondered if there was a reason other than her career that had shaped Jenna's decision not to have children but now, sitting here at a traffic light, was the first time it occurred to him that she might feel differently about having a child that wasn't her own in her life.

That it was just possible she might welcome it?

Ollie would adore Jenna. She was funny and smart and clever and she could connect with children effortlessly.

Good grief...was he actually thinking the unthinkable? That there might be a future for him and Jenna?

Mitch brushed the thought aside as the line of cars ahead of him started to move and it was raining hard enough for his automatic wipers to speed up. One step at a time, he told himself. This thing could fizzle out as quickly as it had begun. But if it didn't... well...who knew?

* * *

It wasn't the first time that Jenna and Mitch had been despatched as first responders to a cardiac arrest and they both knew they could work seamlessly for the intense period of trying to resuscitate someone who was hovering much closer to death than life. To do it in the middle of a building site, with the man's employees trying to hold tarpaulins over the medics, certainly made it more of a challenge as they performed CPR, got the electrodes in place and then defibrillated their patient but it also made it more satisfying to have brought him back to a perfusing rhythm by the time the first available ambulance back-up arrived to transport the man to hospital.

Cranking up the heat in the rapid response vehicle to full strength helped dry Mitch and Jenna's wet clothing and warm them up on the way to their next call which was a multi-vehicle crash. The traffic was backed up for miles around the scene by the time they got near the area and even Jenna's inventive driving tricks couldn't have got them through without the assistance of police units forcing a way through for a fire truck.

They got wet again all too quickly as they

moved between the vehicles involved to triage at least a dozen people but, while some people involved in the accident would need transport to hospital for moderate injuries, nobody was seriously hurt which meant that the rapid response vehicle could leave the scene and be available for the next call.

Jenna's dark curls were plastered against her forehead as she climbed back into the driver's seat and she could feel drips rolling down her neck.

'The weather's vile,' she declared, reaching to unclip the microphone on the dashboard to radio through their availability. 'Had enough yet?'

'Nope.' He was grinning back at her. 'I'm loving it. Bit of rain has never melted anybody that I've heard of.'

He held her gaze when he'd stopped speaking and, for some reason, Jenna's finger resisted pushing the button on the microphone to open communication. Mitch clearly *was* loving this but there was another very clear message in his eyes and it wasn't just the challenging work conditions that were making him so happy.

It was because he was with *her*.

That briefest of moments was enough to

let Jenna know she felt the same way. More importantly, that this was what she'd wanted all along and that, despite convincing herself that it was only something physical missing from her life, she was actually ready for a lot more than that.

As scary as it was, she was ready to embrace life again. Because holding Mitch's gaze for another heartbeat was long enough for questions to be both asked and answered.

Are you thinking what I'm thinking?

Yes.

Can we trust this?

Yes...

They both broke that eye contact then, as if they needed privacy to absorb that something huge was changing here. Jenna sucked in a breath and pushed the button on the side of the microphone.

'Rapid Response One to Control. We're available.'

'Roger that' came the response. 'You can head back to station.'

'Yay...' Jenna started the engine. 'Let's stop at that nice coffee shop on the way and get some cake as well. I reckon we deserve it, don't you?'

'Absolutely.'

But Mitch was pulling his phone from his pocket, something he never normally did when they were working together. Jenna didn't need to catch the frown on his face a second later as he read a text message—she could feel the sudden tension in his body.

'Something up?'

'It's, ah…from my father. He wants me to ring him when I've got a spare moment.' Mitch sounded hesitant. 'He wouldn't ask unless it was something urgent.'

'Call him.' Jenna nodded. 'We're only on our way back to base.'

But she could still sense his hesitation and, oddly, this felt like a much bigger decision than to respond to his father's text message.

Maybe Mitch's father was unwell. Or was he calling about another member of the family, like his mother or siblings? Being reminded that she knew nothing about Mitch's life should be a warning bell but, oddly, it wasn't worrying Jenna at all. She knew *him* now and instinct told her that that was enough. That she could trust him.

She killed the engine and then turned her head. 'I don't want my partner being distracted by a family concern on the next job,' she said. 'We've got time. Call him. I'll do our paperwork.'

It was still raining heavily outside their vehicle and there were people shouting and heavy trucks revving as breakdown services arrived to start clearing the traffic jam but, inside their car, Jenna could still hear the voice of the older man on the other end of Mitch's phone call clearly enough to make out most of what he was saying.

'Sorry to call you like this,' he'd started.

'What's happened, Dad?' Mitch asked quickly. 'What's going on?'

'Nothing to worry about. I just took Ollie in to see Euan, that's all. He was jumping in puddles on the way to school and tripped over. He got a cut on his eyebrow that bled enough to need some attention.'

'Did it need stitching?'

'No, no…nothing like that. Euan just used a couple of those wound closure strips but the bleeding had already stopped by then. I wouldn't even be telling you but Ollie just wanted to tell you about it when you weren't busy. I think he got a bit of a fright, that's all. He needs his dad to tell him how brave he was.'

Jenna wasn't deliberately eavesdropping.

She couldn't even hear the other end of the conversation that clearly but she caught the word 'Dad' and there was no mistaking the bell-like tones of the young child that started speaking then.

'Daddy? I fell over and hurt my head.'

'I know, buddy.' There was a note in Mitch's voice that Jenna had never heard before. 'But Grandy told me how brave you were. I'm really, really proud of you.' He was speaking quietly but the sound was as comforting as a hug. The sound of pure love.

Jenna knew that tone so, so well. The sound of a parent speaking to their child and it cut into a place in her heart with such unexpected sharpness she actually caught her breath and had to blink back a sting behind her eyes that could have become tears. She was perfectly in control by the time Mitch finished his call only a short time later.

She was also hurt.

Disappointed.

And angry. It felt like she had been deceived. Lured into a new hope that her life could include a fairy-tale new direction that provided companionship and love and…and a passion she'd never expected to find again and now it was being taken away from her. Or rather, she had to get rid of it.

As fast as possible.

Her tone, when she spoke, couldn't have been more the opposite to that warmth with which Mitch had been talking to his son.

'So…' Jenna didn't look up from the clipboard on her lap where she had been filling in some paperwork. 'You've got a son?'

'Yeah…' She could hear Mitch take in a slow breath. 'His name's Ollie. He's four.'

As if this new information wasn't devastating enough, Jenna was aware of another alarm sounding.

'And Ollie's mother?' She glanced sideways, only to find that Mitch was staring straight ahead through the rain-streaked windscreen. 'Do you think it might be time to admit that you're married as well?'

'God, *no*…' His gaze swerved to meet hers. 'Ollie's mother died a couple of days after he was born. Good grief…' Mitch pushed his fingers through his hair. 'Do you really think I'd would have gone to bed with you if I was *married*? That I would cheat on someone?'

Jenna shrugged, looking away. She didn't want to see that shock in his eyes. To see that he might have reason to feel hurt himself. 'You didn't tell me you had a kid.'

'No.'

The agreement was a single word that fell into a silence. One that Jenna wasn't about to break because she knew she might say something she would later regret. Or maybe she didn't want Mitch to know how hurt she was. Or that she had even been dreaming of their 'arrangement' growing into something a whole heap more meaningful. At least, this way, she could get out of this with some dignity still intact.

She should start the car and get them back to the station as quickly as possible. That way she could get out of this vehicle and wouldn't have to be this physically close to him because that was becoming harder as the minutes ticked on. She was never going to get really close to this man again, was she? She was never going to be kissed by him again. Or feel that incredible touch…

She was reaching for the key when Mitch broke the silence and her fingers turned into a fist and dropped back to her side.

'I didn't tell you because I knew how you felt about kids. I thought it would put you off having anything to do with me.'

'You got something right, at least.' Jenna's tone was clipped. Icy. 'If I'd known, I'd never have…'

Her words trailed off because it was all too easy to sense that her response was surprising Mitch. Disappointing him? Was he also starting to feel angry, perhaps?

'What—invited me to come out on a shift with you? To get professional experience? You only did that because you fancied some *sex*?'

'No…of course not.' Jenna was appalled.

'So what possible difference could it have made that I was a father?'

The suggestion that she'd offered him the opportunity to work with her in exchange for sex was beyond offensive. And, okay, she wasn't the only one angry, here, but that accusation hurt.

Of course it wouldn't have made any difference that someone she had a professional relationship with was a father. But getting close enough to have sex with anyone had been a very big deal. Something she'd believed had been significant for both of them. Was it really only a matter of minutes ago that she'd been so certain she wasn't the only one who'd thought it could grow into something more? He'd known how she felt about including children in her life so, yeah…he *should* have been more honest. *She* wasn't the one who'd lied by omission.

This was her own fault, however, because she'd allowed herself to start dreaming of a potential future. She'd set herself up for getting hurt and, for heaven's sake, that had been the one thing she'd vowed never to do ever again.

'I made a mistake,' she said aloud. 'A big mistake…'

'You and me both.'

The anger crackled in the air between them. The sooner they could get back to station, the better. Presumably, Mitch would choose to cut this shift short at that point and go home. It was quite likely that Jenna would never see him again.

Good, she thought. She could do without this kind of angst in her life.

As if it was an extension of the atmosphere within the vehicle, the radio crackled into life.

'Control to Rapid Response One. Are you receiving?'

'Receiving.' Jenna had the microphone in her hand instantly. 'Go ahead, Control.'

'Please proceed to four-three-three Andersons Road, towards Fairleigh. Details coming through now. Code Blue, thanks. Collapsed person—not breathing.'

Jenna started the engine. The windscreen wipers sprang back to life and cleared the windscreen as both she and Mitch reached to fasten their seatbelts. The priority call they were being dispatched to was in the opposite direction to the station so it would appear that they had at least one more job they were going to have to work on together. It didn't matter how upsetting their interaction had just been, they were both going to have to forget it completely and think about the patient they were heading towards.

Hearing the wail of the siren made it easy because it was an automatic switch in Jenna's brain that allowed her to dismiss anything personal that could affect her ability as a paramedic.

Maybe Mitch had learned the same lesson during his time as an emergency department consultant. Not that it mattered. He might not have found their conversation anywhere near as disturbing as she had but if anything emotional did affect his work he could go back to the vehicle and stay there for the duration of the call-out, couldn't he?

This was Jenna's vehicle.

Jenna's rules.

CHAPTER SIX

SOMETHING FELT OFF about this job.

It wasn't simply due to the exchange that had clearly ended whatever personal stuff had been going on between him and Jenna. This was something that was sounding an instinctive, professional alarm at the back of Mitch's mind. Something that was making the hairs on the back of his neck prickle as they stood up.

It was an ordinary enough looking house up a long, tree-lined drive. There hadn't been anyone waiting anxiously outside for help to arrive, to direct them to where they were needed, but that wasn't surprising either because the call had warned them that someone wasn't breathing. The person who'd called for the emergency services might be inside the house, as the only person available to perform CPR.

Neither Mitch nor Jenna were giving a single moment's thought to any personal tension between them as they loaded themselves with the gear they'd need to deal with a respiratory or cardiac arrest. The defibrillator, the pack with the IV gear, airway kit and all the drugs they might need, an oxygen cylinder and a suction unit. Both the driveway and the area outside the house had a patchy layer of pebbles and the rain was turning bare ground into mud which Mitch was trying to avoid getting onto his boots. Not that it really mattered—any relatives of someone who needed resuscitation were unlikely to complain about mud being tracked into a house by the people who were arriving to help.

'Ambulance,' Jenna called out as she opened the front door following a sharp rap.

There was no response to the call and they stepped inside to find an eerie silence in the house. That was when Mitch knew something wasn't right. Jenna obviously felt it as well because she paused before going any further into the dark hallway.

'I'll go first,' she murmured, her voice low enough not to be overheard. 'I'm not sure I like this.'

'Same.' Mitch nodded. He reached for a

light switch. 'Being this dark in here's not helping.'

'Keep doors open and an escape route in mind at all times,' Jenna continued whispering. 'And hold that pack in front of you. If you need to, throw it at someone to give you a bit more time to get out.'

But there was no one presenting any kind of threat in the first room they looked into. Or in any of the other rooms that opened off this hallway until they came to a living area at the end. There didn't appear to be anyone in here, either. No one standing, anyway. There was a figure on the floor. A large man was face down and unmoving amongst overturned chairs. A broken plate and spilled food lay beside him on the floor and another half-eaten meal on the table looked as if it had been interrupted some time ago.

Jenna didn't rush in to check on the collapsed person, however. She was looking around. Doors from this room opened into what looked like a kitchen and a back door to the house was open. Rain had puddled onto a tiled floor and, as Mitch followed her gaze, the wind caught the door which made it bang shut and then bounce open again.

'Stay by the door,' Jenna told Mitch. 'Keep

an eye out for anyone coming in through the front.'

She walked slowly towards the prone male figure. With gloved fingers she felt the side of his neck and for what seemed like a long, long moment, she was completely still. She lifted her gaze to meet Mitch's and gave her head a small shake. Then she reached for her radio with her other hand. It was then that Mitch noticed the blood on the hand she'd used to feel for a pulse and he could see the shadow of the dark stain on the carpet beside the man's head.

'Rapid Response One to Control. Are you receiving?'

'Receiving loud and clear. Go ahead.'

'We have a situation at four-three-three Andersons Road. Code zero male.'

Mitch knew that the code zero was used as a status for a deceased person. He assumed that Jenna was quite sure that he had been deceased for enough time to make an attempt to resuscitate him futile. She used another code he wasn't familiar with and he wondered if that was to indicate that the circumstances looked more than a little suspicious. Just as he wondered if a person responsible for this death might have been the one who'd made the call to the emergency services, something to one side of the room caught his attention. Someone was outside, looking through the window, but they were already rapidly moving out of sight as Mitch looked up.

'Someone's outside,' he warned Jenna.

'We're not alone on scene,' Jenna informed the person in the control centre. 'We require police back-up. Stat.'

'Roger that.' The radio fell silent for a few moments, as though the call taker was busy activating other calls. Jenna was on her feet as it crackled back to life.

'Return to your vehicle if it's safe to do so. Don't touch anything and don't leave the scene. Back-up will be with you as soon as possible.'

'Roger that.'

Mitch waited for instruction from Jenna before he moved.

'Try and keep to the same track we used coming in here,' she told him quietly. 'If this *is* a homicide, forensics will be all over this and we don't want to have interfered with any more evidence than we might have already.' She way she shook her head showed Mitch she was less than happy. 'I've heard about cases like this. We could be stuck here for hours.'

* * *

The wheels of the car hadn't sunk into the layer of mud at the top of the driveway but they might as well have been buried up to their rims.

They were stuck.

The property in Andersons Road had ghost-like figures everywhere. Forensic investigators wearing disposable white overalls with hoods, masks, gloves and shoe covers were coming and going from the house and working outside in the rain, trying to collect evidence before it got destroyed by weather conditions or movements of people or vehicles.

Mitch and Jenna couldn't drive away. They were waiting for their fingerprints to be taken so they could be excluded from prints that would be taken inside the house and currently they had only socks on their feet because their boots had been borrowed to record the kind of tracks they may have made going into or coming out of the house, where it had been confirmed that a murder had taken place some hours ago.

Listening to the chatter of emergency services radio transmissions only made it more frustrating that a rapid response vehicle had been taken off the road and its crew stood down for the rest of this shift. There was no indication of when they might be allowed to leave and it already felt like far too long, thanks to the fact that Jenna and Mitch were barely talking to each other.

Any distraction had been effectively diluted and the silence inside this vehicle was loaded with all the angst of the conversation they'd been having when the call to this incident had happened.

Mitch was still feeling that edge of anger. With himself as much as with Jenna. How had he allowed himself to think it was okay to simply ignore the existence of his own son just because he'd found a woman he was so attracted to? He'd already known that Jenna's attitude towards children meant that she would never be someone he would want to have involved in his day-to-day personal life but what had happened between them had felt significant in its own way. And she'd dismissed it as being a 'big mistake'? That stung.

But it wasn't entirely Jenna's fault, was it?

He'd known he was being less than completely honest and he hadn't liked that, either. A sideways glance showed him that Jenna was watching the forensic team at work but he knew she wasn't happy. She'd rather be anywhere else than stuck in the small space of this vehicle with him. Not talking to each other wasn't helping, either. It was, in fact, rather immature behaviour, come to think of it.

'I'm sorry,' he found himself saying aloud—and meaning it. 'I don't like things being like this between us.'

Jenna's head turned swiftly. She looked almost relieved. 'Neither do I,' she said quietly. 'It's horrible.'

'I should have been more honest with you.'

Jenna didn't say anything but Mitch had seen the flash of hurt in the instant before she dropped her gaze. It clearly needed a bit more than just an apology to fix an atmosphere he knew neither of them wanted to be sitting in for goodness only knew how much longer.

'I didn't expect you to offer me the chance to work with you like this,' he continued. 'And I certainly didn't expect to be attracted to you like I was and…and to find that you felt the same way was… I don't know…a kind of miracle. I didn't stop to think about anything else.'

He hadn't been thinking of anything except how much he wanted to be physically close to Jenna. A closeness that was never likely to happen again, now.

'I didn't think that my home life was relevant to anything happening between me and you,' he added. 'It wasn't as if we were dating. Or thinking about a serious relationship.'

'No.'

Jenna seemed to be staring at her hands as she responded in almost a whisper but then she glanced up and met his gaze. Just for a moment. Just long enough to remind Mitch of the way she'd held his gaze for much longer than that only a very short time ago and that he'd been quite certain that he wasn't the only one to be thinking that this—whatever it was they'd discovered together—could possibly become something more than putting a toe back into the waters of a long abandoned sex life. And then she spoke again.

'I'm sorry, too,' she said. 'I know I overreacted.'

'I doubt that,' Mitch said. 'I'm pretty sure that whatever it is that's made you feel so strongly about things is completely justified.'

Silence fell again but, this time, it was different. Mitch could sense that Jenna wanted to say something but didn't know where to start. Or whether she should say anything at all, perhaps? The only way he could help was to give her the time she needed and, sure enough, a minute or so later, she began offering words that were hesitant enough to sound as if they were coming from a very private and well-guarded place.

'I...had a son, too,' she told him, slowly. 'His name was Eli. He was four years old when he died.'

Oh... *God*... The same age as Oliver? Mitch couldn't bear to even try and imagine how devastating it would be to lose his child. How impossible it would be to carry on any semblance of a normal life.

'Oh... Jenna,' he said, softly. 'I'm *so*, so sorry,'

Reaching for her hand had been purely instinctive. That she let him take hold of it and curled her fingers around his was a response that made the crack in his heart widen. He could feel the enormity of what she had faced. Could feel the astonishing amount of courage she had needed.

The silence this time was totally different. It felt as if they were connecting on a new level. It reminded Mitch of the feeling of making up after a heated argument. Jenna still hadn't taken her hand away.

'You know what it's like,' she said. 'To lose someone you love. You said that Ollie's mother died just after he was born?'

'Mmm.' Mitch was very aware of the subtle pressure of Jenna's hand. An invitation to share? Would that open the door to hearing more of *her* story? Mitch wanted to know more—as much as she was willing to tell him.

'Tegan developed signs of pre-eclampsia,' he told her. 'She had an emergency Caesarean at thirty-one weeks but…there were complications.' He took a slow, inward breath. It wasn't often he needed to recall details that were still horrific because it was so unexpected, these days, to lose a young, healthy woman due to childbirth. 'Her blood pressure was still way too high. Her liver had a spontaneous rupture. She went into renal failure.' Mitch swallowed hard. 'She never saw Ollie. Never held him.'

'So *that's* why you gave up your position as HOD at St Barnabas?' Jenna's tone was one of complete understanding.

'My life imploded.' Mitch nodded. 'The only thing that mattered was Ollie and I had time while he was in the NICU to rearrange my life around him. My dad was the rock that let me hold things together. I eventually moved back into the house I'd grown up in—with my son. I'd planned to take a year off work but then the position at the medical centre came up and I thought, why not? Being a GP would make me part of the community and the hours can be very child friendly for a single parent.'

He could feel the way Jenna's hand had relaxed in his as she listened to him. And she still hadn't taken it away? He gave it a tiny squeeze. 'You'd know about how important that is, I'm guessing? Or was Eli's dad around to help?'

Jenna shook her head. 'That was where it started. Stefan was a paramedic like me— we met when we were rostered on the same watch—and, after Eli was born, we juggled shifts so that one of us could be at home with him as much as possible. Eli was about six months old when Stef had taken him for a walk to the park and he got hit by a car that went out of control and onto the footpath.

Hit and run. They never caught the driver.'
Mitch heard the tiny hiccup in her voice.

'Stef died before an ambulance even got
there but a witness said he'd done his best to
protect Eli by trying to push him out of the
way in his pram. That he kept asking about
him until he lost consciousness completely.'

Mitch simply nodded. He would do anything to protect Ollie. Any father would.

'It undoubtedly saved his life but he still
had some serious injuries, including a skull
fracture. He was in hospital for more than a
month and…and he developed epilepsy later
that was hard to control with medication. It
was a seizure that he died from. Nobody at
school saw it start and he was in the playground. They think he just hit his head too
hard, too many times, on the asphalt.'

Mitch didn't have to say anything to let
Jenna know that he was thinking of his own
son and imagining her unbearable loss. All
he needed to do was to hold her hand. And
to hold her gaze, eventually, when she was
ready to meet his.

'How long ago did you lose Eli?'

'Nearly five years now. Which was about
when I came up with the idea of the FRAME
network and threw myself into getting the

project off the ground. My career was all I had left, you know?'

'I know,' Mitch said quietly. 'And you've achieved something amazing but...'

Jenna's eyes widened. *'But?'*

'But I think you're lonely. Like me...'

Jenna's lips parted as if she was about to say something but then they were both startled by a tap on the window behind her. Her head swerved and she rolled the window down enough to hear what the white-shrouded person was saying.

'We've finished with your boots. And we reckon we've got anything useful we can find out here in the way of tyre marks and shoe prints. Whatever's left is getting ruined by this rain. Sorry to have held you guys up for so long.'

'No worries,' Jenna told him.

Mitch nodded his head. He was glad they'd been trapped on scene. If they hadn't, they would have gone back to the station and he would have gone home and he and Jenna would most likely have never seen each other again. Ever. Instead, they had just discovered a kind of connection they would probably never be able to find with anyone else on the planet.

An astonishing connection.

'We still need to get your fingerprints but the team's flat out inside the house. Would it be okay if you went into the nearest police station and did it there?'

'Of course. We've got one virtually next door to our headquarters in Croydon. Would that be okay?'

'Absolutely. I'll get in touch with them and let them know you're coming.'

Jenna had been about to deny that she was lonely when that extraordinary conversation with Mitch had been interrupted but she'd had time to think about it on the drive back to her home patch.

She was still thinking about it as she watched Mitch take his turn to have his fingerprints recorded. Focusing on his hands reminded her of how it had felt to have him holding her hand while they were sharing such intimate details of their personal histories. And how it had felt to have him touch her—and hold her—in a way that she hadn't been touched, or held, in such a very long time.

As if he sensed the direction of her thoughts, Mitch looked up and caught her gaze at that point and Jenna felt the corners of her mouth lift. No more than a hint of a smile, really, but it was enough to make the corners of Mitch's eyes crinkle and create a softening in his expression that was almost like the kind of touch Jenna had been thinking about.

He waited until they were outside the police station and walking back to the ambulance station where Jenna had parked the car before saying anything.

'Just so you know,' he told her, 'you didn't overreact. I think I blindsided you in a way that must have been an absolute kick in the guts and I just want to say "I'm sorry" again.'

It was still raining. Mitch was holding an umbrella over both of them as they walked side by side.

'I kind of did overreact,' Jenna said. 'I can actually deal with kids perfectly well when they're my patients or my friends' children. I think…' Mitch was an amazing person and he deserved to know the truth, didn't he? 'I think I read too much into what was happening with our…um…friendship and that's why it hit me so hard. I could never get close to a child again. I think my ability to love anyone so unconditionally died when Eli died.'

Mitch nodded slowly. 'I get that. I've felt like that about sharing my life with another woman since I lost Tegan.'

The long glance they shared acknowledged the sad connection they'd found in each other.

'But I think you're right,' Jenna added quietly. 'I hadn't really thought about it but I *have* been lonely.' She smiled at him and made an attempt to lighten the atmosphere. 'Maybe I should get a dog, after all.'

'I've got a dog, too.' Mitch returned the smile. 'I just wanna be totally upfront about that one.'

Jenna's smile widened but Mitch's actually faded. 'I really like you, Jenna,' he said.

'I really like you, too, Mitch.'

'And, I have to say, the sex has been amazing. *You're* amazing.'

'Same...' Jenna had to drop her gaze to escape the intensity in Mitch's gaze. She remembered how she had felt when it seemed like she was never going to see Mitch again. How deeply that hurt and disappointment had reached.

'We know where we stand, don't we? And

we can probably understand *why* we feel like that better than anyone else would.'

Jenna nodded her agreement.

'And…we're both lonely.'

Jenna nodded again. She couldn't disagree with that.

'Maybe…' he suggested softly, 'we can still be friends? With zero expectations of anything else? Even better friends than we were because…you know…no more secrets.'

They were almost at the station where Mitch's car was parked. They were also close to Jenna's flat.

'It's early,' she said. 'But they'll have someone else covering the rapid response and they won't put us back on duty for less than a couple of hours.' She looked up to catch Mitch's gaze. 'Do you need to rush home?'

He shook his head. 'They won't be expecting me until the usual time. Ollie's perfectly happy with his grandpa. He just wanted me to know how brave he'd been.'

'So, would you like to come back to my place? For…a coffee or something?'

Mitch hadn't looked away and, if she'd thought his gaze had been intense before, it was nothing compared to what she could see in his eyes right now.

'I would like that very much,' he said.

Mitch was tilting the umbrella so that it became a screen from anyone else in the street. He was also bending his head and Jenna knew he was about to kiss her. And she wanted him to. More than anything.

'I choose the something,' he murmured, as his lips brushed hers before settling. 'If that's all good with you.'

That did it. That private code after the intensity of how they'd forged a new level to their connection made the thought of not having Mitch in her life—or in her bed—something she didn't want to even contemplate.

Jenna felt his lips against hers, his mouth swallowing her response.

'Couldn't be better…'

CHAPTER SEVEN

MITCH HAD FALLEN ASLEEP.

This wasn't part of the new routine of the last few weeks and Jenna knew she should wake him up and she would. Soon. But he'd had such an early start to get to Croydon for the beginning of his weekly shift with her in the rapid response vehicle at seven a.m. It had been a full-on day, as well, with back-to-back call-outs until six p.m. and, even now, at nearly eight-thirty p.m., there would probably be significant traffic on the roads between Croydon and Allensbury so the drive would be safer if he just had a bit of a cat-nap. Ten or fifteen minutes at the most so he wouldn't be too late home.

Not that Ollie would still be awake, of course, but Mitch had had a chat to him on the phone to say goodnight and he was perfectly happy at home with his grandpa. And Jenna had been perfectly happy to hear the conversation on speakerphone because she'd made the mental shift since that awful day when they had almost thrown away their friendship. Ollie was a child like any other in her life. The offspring of one of her friends. Or a patient. She could keep her guardrails firmly in place.

It was all good.

Jenna felt her mouth curve into a contented smile as she snuggled a little closer to Mitch, turning her face just enough to touch that soft skin on the underside of his arm with her lips. Mitch stirred in his sleep, making a soft sound and curling his arm around Jenna to draw her even closer. She closed her eyes and let her breath out slowly in a soft sigh.

Actually, it couldn't be better, could it?

Thanks to that intense day when she'd discovered Mitch was a father and had finally opened up about the reason it had upset her so much, there was a new connection that felt way more than 'good'. He understood. He been through a huge loss himself. Jenna didn't have to hide anything any longer and neither did Mitch so there was a new honesty there as well. An honesty that extended to them being totally upfront about what they wanted from their friendship.

Jenna was never going to be asked to include Ollie in her life in any meaningful way. The last thing Mitch wanted was a wife—or a new mother for his son—for exactly the same reasons that having another child was the last thing Jenna wanted. What Mitch *did* want was a connection with someone that could fill the space where loneliness took up residence. Jenna was more than happy to be that someone because now she didn't have to keep *doing* things or *going* places so that she wouldn't notice she was right in the middle of that lonely space herself.

And, yes, she did have other friends she could be with, as company to go out to dinner or a show or simply to hang with, but it wasn't the same because there were levels to loneliness and one of them could only be filled by a physical closeness that none of Jenna's friends could ever provide and she'd never wanted to go looking for it elsewhere.

She hadn't been looking for it when Mitch had walked into her life.

She hadn't known how much she needed it, either. That closeness. His touch. And the sex…well, she wouldn't have believed it could get any better but there was a tenderness to it now that could only have come from that understanding—that unique connection of shared loss that they had with each other.

Mitch stirred again and Jenna could feel the moment he woke up, as his muscles tensed and he drew in a sharp breath.

'Oh, no...what time is it?'

'Only eight-thirty. Don't worry, you've only been asleep for about ten minutes.'

She could feel the tension in his body ebbing. 'Phew... I had a horrible thought that I wouldn't get home before Ollie got up.' Mitch rolled onto his side and smiled at Jenna. 'We have important plans for after breakfast and before I go into work to cover the Saturday morning clinic. I'd better get up and dressed.'

'Okay...' Jenna was smiling back at him. 'I *was* going to wake you up soon but I thought you could do with the rest before you have to make that long trip home. And...'

'And...?'

Her smile felt almost shy, which was a bit crazy considering what they'd been doing only a very short time ago. 'And it was rather nice just lying here with you for a few minutes.'

'Mmm…' Mitch bent his head and placed a gentle kiss on Jenna's lips. 'I'd better not tell you how much I look forward to my Fridays these days.'

He kissed her again and, this time, she could feel those first flickers of desire building again—a sensation she was coming to recognise instantly and welcome more than wholeheartedly. Maybe Mitch was feeling it too, because he broke off the kiss with a soft groan.

'I really have to go.' He rolled away from Jenna to sit on the side of the bed. He reached for the shirt that had been thrown carelessly over the wooden post, pushed his arms through the sleeves and began to button it up.

Jenna pulled the sheet up to cover her bare breasts as she propped herself against her pillows to watch Mitch get dressed.

'What are the important plans with Ollie?' There…she'd included his son in their conversation without even thinking about it. As if it was the most natural thing in the world. It was getting easier all the time.

'It's Pets' Day at school soon and Ollie wants to take our old dog, Jet. What he's most excited about is that there's a dress-up competition for pets. Ollie's been dressing him up in weird things like hats and jumpers ever since he was a toddler and Jet is an extremely tolerant dog.' Mitch had pulled on his underwear and picked up the formal dark trousers he wore to work with her. 'It should be great fun.'

'I'm guessing Jet is a black dog?'

Mitch threw her a grin. 'Yep. A rather overweight, sixteen-year-old black Lab.'

'And what's he going to be dressed up as?'

His socks were going on now. 'A doctor.'

Jenna laughed. 'Whose idea was that? Yours or Ollie's?'

'It got decided at a family conference. But it's me that has to figure out how to make a white coat for him. We're taking the measurements in the morning and my wonderful receptionist, Josie, is going to help cut it out and sew it. We found an ancient coat in our supply room. Nobody wears them these days, do they? Josie reckons we could get clever and cut it to keep the collar and buttons.' Mitch looked up from lacing his boots to smile at Jenna. 'I've got a broken stethoscope, too. I reckon Jet will be quite happy to have that hanging round his neck.'

'He's bound to win,' Jenna said. She was still chuckling. 'I'd love to see it.'

'So why don't you come along?' Mitch's tone was casual as he stood up but he was holding her gaze carefully. 'It's on Wednesday. Didn't I hear you tell someone on station that it's your day off next week?'

Oh…it was one thing to find it perfectly natural to be talking to Mitch about his son but the prospect of meeting the little boy was something else altogether.

And Mitch clearly knew what a big ask it was. He didn't say anything but he sat back on the edge of the bed and pulled Jenna, wrapped in the sheet, into his arms. He still didn't say anything. He simply held her and pressed his lips against the top of her head.

It felt like an apology.

It felt like he understood exactly how hard that might be for her.

It also felt like he really, really cared about how she was feeling.

Mitch's arms tightened around her. 'Don't say anything,' he whispered into her hair. 'Just think about it.'

Jenna hadn't needed to be told to 'think about it'.

It was hard to think about anything else, in fact. Especially when she had several hours' drive ahead of her to get to Sheffield, where she was booked to take a FRAME refresher course for rural GPs. She'd had meetings during the day for final editing on the new set of clinical guidelines for their practitioners so it was mid-afternoon by the time she set off and it was only then that Jenna realised she'd missed lunch. Maybe that was why it was harder to focus on her driving and contributing to the reason her thoughts kept circling back to the invitation to attend Pets' Day that Mitch had issued that evening last week.

Food might help. Coffee certainly would, so Jenna pulled in to the next service area off the motorway—one of those vast places that had everything from petrol stations to motels with enough restaurants, fast food outlets and even bars or supermarkets to cater for any possible refreshment travellers might desire. With coffee already on her tray, Jenna was heading for a place where you could choose your own sandwich fillings when she passed something far more tempting.

Potato skins. Hot, crispy, cheesy potato skins were exactly what she needed right now and Jenna ordered a plateful and then carried her tray to search for an empty table to sit and enjoy her meal. It wasn't until after she sat down and took her first bite that she realised she might have made a bit of a mistake. For one thing, as soon as she tasted the potato skin, she was taken back to that night in the pub with Mitch and his classmates at the end of their course. The night that had ended with them making love.

The night that had changed her life.

The follow-on from that was, of course, remembering the last occasion they'd spent together in bed and how *that* had ended, with Mitch holding her so tenderly after inviting her to come on what could only be considered a family kind of occasion.

Actually, there was a third thing that Jenna noticed as she swallowed that first mouthful. The only available table she'd been able to find was on the edge of a children's play area. Just outside, through wide, open doors there were seesaws and swings, a wooden fort with a slide from the highest point and climbing towers joined by swing bridges with rope walls. Inside, there were parents all around her, feeding young children or enjoying a coffee and break themselves as they watched their offspring let off steam in the playground.

It was Family Central. For a moment, Jenna considered loading her food and drink back onto the tray and going in search of another place to sit. Back in her vehicle, even? No, she told herself firmly. That was ridiculous. There was no reason to move. She'd been dealing with seeing families and children for years without falling apart so why would anything have suddenly become too difficult now?

Her gaze drifted to settle on a young mother who was breastfeeding a baby as she ate a hamburger and fries with one hand. Her partner was also eating his meal one-handed as he pushed a stroller back and forth with his other hand. The toddler in the stroller was sucking her thumb, her eyes almost shut, on the verge of falling asleep.

The clarity of the time-slip in Jenna's head—and her heart—was startling. She could almost feel that soft, warm weight of Eli in her own arms as she breastfed him, sometimes dipping her head to kiss that wispy hair and just soak in the smell of him. That delicious scent of milkiness and warmth and baby shampoo. She could even feel the echo of the exhaustion of those days along with that extraordinary difference that going from a couple to become a family had created.

She could feel a poignant smile tilting her lips as she remembered how happy she and Stefan had been. How there were those moments when the love was so huge it was overwhelming. How, even then, when she'd had no idea of what was just around the corner in her life, she'd felt afraid of the idea of losing it all.

Jenna shifted her gaze to stare, unseeing, through the doors to the playground. She was remembering Stefan now and the way he would rock Eli to sleep in his pushchair while listening to music through his ear buds, or reading a book with one hand. A clever, quick, passionate young man, Stefan had loved to dance. And argue about almost anything. So different to Mitch, who was mature and thoughtful and had a kindness and empathy that could only come from experiencing the hard parts of life.

Mitch made her feel safe but Stefan…well, the light had gone out in her life when Stefan had died and what made it so much worse, if that was possible, was that she had to grieve for him as she sat, day after day, in the paediatric intensive care unit beside Eli's bed as he slowly began to recover from his own injuries.

The potato skins were getting cold on the plate but Jenna had forgotten about her food. Her eyes were focusing on what was going on outside now. She could see parents holding young children on a seesaw where the seats were on the backs of large, wooden ducks. The toddlers were laughing with delight as they bounced up and down. Her journey with Eli had had moments like that as part of the rollercoaster. He could be a laughing, singing child one minute and then, in the blink of an eye, he would be unresponsive and on the ground or floor, convulsing. There had been a new fear to live with then, on top of what should have been the worst thing that could have happened when her fledging family had been ripped apart by losing Stefan.

Eli had only been four years old. Jenna found herself doing something she hadn't done for years—letting her gaze search until she found a child that would be about that age. He'd be nearly nine years old now if he'd lived. That was the next automatic search mode and…yes…those boys who were scrambling across the swing bridges would be somewhere between eight and ten years old but she only watched them for a few seconds. It didn't feel meaningful. Eli would be only four years old for ever in her head. And her heart.

Ollie was four years old.

If Jenna went to his school for Pets' Day she would not only meet Ollie, she would be with a whole class of other children the same age. Could she really cope with that?

No.

Yes. Of course she could. In the same way she coped with the young patients she treated or played with the children of her friends. Or watched a random bunch of kids playing the way she was doing now.

Did she *want* to cope with that?

No.

Yes.

No, because it might be too hard if it came with this new clarity that felt like a filter, which prevented too much light or something being allowed through, had somehow been lifted. A clarity that felt like a direct connection to the past and all the pain that had come from losing the future she'd believed she had. With her very own family.

She wasn't hungry any longer but Jenna sipped her coffee, looking back towards the young family she'd first noticed. Both the baby and the toddler were fast asleep now and the young parents were smiling at each other. For now, at least, they were coping with travelling with young children. They were winning.

Jenna wanted that. The coping. The winning.

So, the answer was definitely 'yes'. Because she really wanted to be able to cope and not to have to fear those memories. That would be a kind of freedom all by itself, wouldn't it?

And, maybe, she wanted to go to Pets' Day because it was Mitch who had asked her. He knew exactly what he was asking her to face and, as someone who knew all about facing ghosts from the past, he believed that she could cope. A part of her wanted to show him that he was right. Or perhaps she wanted him to be proud of her?

Taking another long look at the playground was deliberate. So was searching out a child of the right age so that she could pretend it was Ollie. She waited for the kind of jolt she'd experienced when she'd first found out that Mitch had a young son but it didn't happen. The pain of Eli's loss didn't come at her like a runaway train either, so something had changed. The shift towards it being easy to talk about Ollie and accept him as part of Mitch's life had taken weeks but this shift seemed to be happening with enough speed to be disconcerting. There was no mistaking it, however. The feeling that she could cope with something like Pets' Day—if she had Mitch beside her. And that being able to cope could be the key to making life better.

Not that she'd ever choose to become a mother again. Or a stepmother, for that matter, but to be able to see life with this sort of clarity, with no need for protective filters to dull what she was seeing couldn't be anything other than a good thing. Imagine if she could actually enjoy being around children instead of simply 'coping' with it? She'd been afraid of getting close enough to another man for a physical relationship, after all, and look at how she felt about Mitch now? She certainly couldn't dismiss the comfort and pleasure and…and the sheer joy he'd brought back into her life.

Jenna already knew she didn't need to hide anything from Mitch—the way she still hid her personal history from anybody new that she met or worked with and…and it felt like her life had been fragmented ever since it had fallen apart eight years ago. As if it had been so broken, it could never be put back together. But that's what this new feeling was. As if Mitch—and Ollie—and maybe even Jet and Pets' Day might somehow be a glue that could bring those pieces of her life back together. If she could be brave enough to trust where this feeling might eventually lead her, who knew how much better her life might become?

Pushing away the plate of cold food, Jenna reached for her phone to send a text message.

I've never been to a Pets' Day. And I've certainly never seen a dog dressed up as a doctor.

Jenna took a deep breath before tapping in her next words.

I'd love to come if that invitation's still open.

Andrew Mitchell was bursting with pride.

It wasn't only because his son was standing in front of Allensbury Primary School's Reception class of twenty pupils giving a talk about his pet, although he was doing a very good job of it.

'Jet's a black dog and he's very, very old.

He's sixteen, which my dad says is like over a hundred years old for a person and…and that's even older than my *grandpa*.'

Ollie's grandpa, Michael Mitchell, was the first to laugh out loud. He shook his head and shared a resigned glance with some of the other adults packed into the back of the classroom. The closest person grinning back at him was Jenna, who'd arrived just in time for the 'interesting things about my pet' presentations—the preparation of which had been the children's reading, writing and art projects for the week. Her gaze shifted to meet Mitch's and the sparkle of amusement was still lighting up those golden brown eyes and making them even warmer than usual. She seemed to be enjoying this, which was rather a big relief because he'd known that, in introducing her to his son, he might be pushing her in a direction she really didn't want to go. Not only that, she was in a classroom full of four-year-old children and that had to be making her heart ache on a level he couldn't begin to know.

Ollie was wrapping up his talk. 'Dogs need food and Jet's favourite thing is toast and peanut butter. And cuddles. And that's why I love my pet…'

Mitch's gaze slid sideways without his head moving so Jenna didn't realise he was looking at her again. He saw the way she caught her bottom lip between her teeth and he could almost feel the increased tension in her body, as if she was bracing herself, and he knew exactly what it was that she was afraid of.

The memories.

The echo of that devastating moment of loss.

But she was smiling again now and joining in the applause as Ollie tugged on Jet's lead and took him to sit on the mat with him.

And that was when Mitch realised the pride that was filling his heart included Jenna as well. He knew how courageous she was—you only had to look at what she'd done with her life in the face of a double tragedy to know that—but she could have avoided this and she hadn't. This was her first ever Pets' Day at a school. Possibly the most full-on exposure to so many children who were the same age as Eli had been when she'd lost him but she was facing it. With dignity and humour and…and that determination to really live every moment of her life that was just one of the admirable things about this woman who'd fallen into his life.

He could feel that pride, laced with his understanding of how hard this might be for Jenna, tightening something in his gut and wrapping itself around his heart. It was a poignant feeling—wanting to take that pain away from someone because he cared about them. Kind of like the way he felt when Ollie got hurt, or sick. Or when he noticed his dad looking tired enough to make it hit home that his father was getting older and wouldn't be around for ever.

People he loved…

This was more than that brief thought he'd had, when he'd seen Jenna with Kirsty at that accident scene, that perhaps there might be a future for himself that included her. Good grief…the way he'd just put his feelings about Jenna up there with Ollie and his dad made it seem as if he was falling in love with her. The thought was so out of left field—unwelcome, even—it could be dismissed in a nanosecond and Mitch could focus on what was actually real, as a small girl with a big smile, her hair in gorgeous cornrows with the braids decorated with beads, got up and carried a shoebox to the front of the class. She took off the lid and lifted out her pet.

'This is my turtle. His name is Winston.'

'That's Mia,' Mitch whispered to Jenna. 'She's Ollie's very best friend.'

They had to sit through several more pet show and tell performances but they were all so cute, nobody minded the squeeze of it being standing room only for the adult audience. Things became a little more dramatic when a cat was making it very clear that it didn't want to be in its carry box by hissing, yowling and trying to scratch its young owner through a gap in the door and a parent had to step in to rescue it. A rabbit got loose in the classroom and a small dog was sick on the carpet. Everybody was more than ready to go outside for some fresh air when they were told the last two class members had their pets tied up on the playing field.

'Oh…' Jenna's jaw dropped as they rounded the corner of the school building. 'Ponies?'

'Allensbury's the centre of a rural community. There are quite a few small farms and lifestyle blocks around here. One of the GPs I work with, Euan, has a smallholding where he keeps a Highland cow. A prize-winning bull, in fact.'

'Really?' Jenna blinked. 'Is it somewhere around here, with one of his kids?'

Mitch shook his head. 'Euan's not remotely interested in having children in his life. Probably why he's still single.'

It occurred to Mitch that Euan might think Jenna was the perfect woman and maybe he should introduce them to each other. The thought that followed, however, was a silent but incredulous huff of dismissal. *As if...*

Jenna was distracted again. 'And there's a donkey over there...' She crossed her hands on her chest in an enchantingly childish gesture of delight. 'I *love* donkeys.'

'I love donkeys too.' Ollie, with Jet plodding patiently beside him, caught up with them, his grandfather right behind him.

'This is Jenna.' Mitch introduced her to his son and father.

Michael's smile was warm and welcoming. Ollie's eyebrows had almost disappeared under the spikes of his hair. 'Are you Daddy's girlfriend?'

Jenna hesitated for a second, shooting a quick glance at Mitch, as if unsure what he might have told Ollie, or more to the point, his father? He hoped his smile was reassuring. There was no pressure here. No expectations—just as they'd agreed.

'A girlfriend is a bit different to a friend, Ollie. Jenna's my friend. And I go and work with her sometimes.'

'But she's a girl.' Ollie looked puzzled. 'And she's your friend. Mia's *my* girlfriend.'

'You're right.' Jenna was smiling now. 'I'm Daddy's friend. Just like Mia is your friend.'

Ollie nodded. He knew he'd been right. 'He told me you were coming. Because you want to see Jet in the fancy dress competition.'

'I do indeed. I can't wait to see Dr Dog.'

Ollie turned to his father. 'Can we put his clothes on now, Daddy?'

'Not yet, buddy. We're going to have lunch first. There's a big sausage sizzle, remember? Don't forget you promised not to let Jet eat too much. We don't want him being sick like Aiden's puppy.' Mitch was looking around. 'Where's Mia?'

'She had to put Winston back in the car. And her mummy said she had to have her puffer before she came near the ponies. In case she's…'llergic.'

'Ah…' Mitch nodded. 'Of course. Mia's asthmatic,' he told Jenna. 'They haven't sorted out what all her triggers are but she did have a serious attack and needed admission to hospital after she had a pony ride last year.'

There were pony rides happening at Pets' Day as part of the activities that were on offer during the relaxed picnic and barbecue lunch. A lot of parents must have taken time off work, Mitch realised, because many children had both parents there, along with siblings who were still too young for school. There was an overwhelmingly family feel to the day and while this was the Mitchell family's first Pets' Day, it still felt very different thanks to having Jenna with them. And he wasn't the only one noticing the difference, it seemed. Mitch was aware of the curious glances coming their way from people who knew him in the community.

He knew they were referred to as 'the Mitchell men'. Three males from three different generations that had forged an unusual family unit after tragedy and people cared about them. He couldn't blame people for being curious, either—this was the first time he'd ever been seen with a female companion in public. He could only hope that Jenna wasn't aware of the interest she was generating, which she might interpret as a level of pressure she would rather avoid.

She certainly seemed to still be enjoying herself. Mia's mother, Hanna, had joined them to sit on the grass on the playing field and she was talking to Jenna about her daughter's asthma.

'The ambulance people were wonderful when they came that first time when she was only ten months old. I was so worried about her.'

'I know. It's such a scary thing when you know your baby's having trouble breathing.'

'They thought it was an infection then. Bronchiolitis?'

'It's the first diagnosis I would have considered myself in a baby.'

'Then they said it was reactive airways disease, but the last attack was so bad she ended up in intensive care and they did a lot of tests and said it's definitely asthma so now we have all the inhalers and spacers and an action plan and even a nebuliser at home.'

'She doesn't look like she's having trouble with all the different animals around her today.' Mitch joined the conversation. 'She and Ollie are having great fun.' He was smiling as he lifted his phone to try and capture the moment in a photograph.

The children were giggling as they rolled around, pulling up handfuls of grass to throw at each other. They both had grubby hands, grass in their hair and smears of tomato sauce on their faces. Jet was taking advantage of the lack of supervision and was crawling over the grass on his stomach to snatch up the half-eaten sausages rolled in bread.

The adults exchanged glances and smiles. No one was about to growl at them for getting messy or forgetting promises not to let the dog eat too much food. This was one of those moments in life. One of the small things that made life as good as it could be. Throwing grass. Laughter. Being with friends and family.

On impulse, Mitch shifted his focus and caught a photo of Jenna watching the children with a smile as big as Mia's on her face. In this moment she didn't look as if she was tormented by past memories at all. She looked like she was loving this. No one who was watching her right now would ever imagine the pain and grief in her past.

Maybe she'd even forgotten it herself in the joy of this moment? No one would think she was afraid of loving anyone like that again, either.

And…maybe…if she got used to it bit by bit, she might forget that herself?

Because that feeling—the one that gave him that knot deep inside and squeezed his heart like a vice—had come back and he couldn't simply dismiss it by distracting himself this time. Especially not when he lowered his phone camera to find Jenna turning towards him, with that gorgeous smile still tilting her lips.

His gaze snagged on those lips and another sensation joined the mix he was aware of as he remembered the softness and taste of Jenna's mouth and what it was like to hold this woman in his arms.

That was all he wanted to do now. To hold her.

To say *I think I'm falling in love with you, Jenna…*

Just as well he couldn't do either of those things here because Jenna would run a mile. He'd be breaking their agreement—the one where they'd both been honest in saying that they didn't want a future with each other that had even the hint of a partnership like marriage. Jenna never wanted to be a mother to someone else's child and Mitch would never risk Ollie's happiness by including anybody in his family that didn't love his son as much as he did.

All he could do was to return Jenna's smile. To be relieved that a bell rang in that moment, signalling the end of the lunch break and that it was time to prepare for the Pets' fancy dress competition and to be thankful that it hadn't been a huge drama for Jenna to join a family occasion.

Because that was what it felt like.

Family...

CHAPTER EIGHT

'HE'S BRADYCARDIC.' JENNA had had her fingers on the man's wrist even as she greeted the patient they'd been called to see. Her glance up at Mitch was brief. 'Let's get some leads on for an ECG.' She turned back to the man, who was slumped on a bench seat in the waiting area of this barber's shop. 'How are you feeling, Bruce? Apart from the chest pain?'

'A bit dizzy. And…like I might be going to be sick.'

The barber stepped back swiftly. 'I'll find a bowl,' he said.

'Thanks.' Jenna looked up at the onlookers, a couple of whom were still wearing capes that suggested their haircuts and shaves had been interrupted. 'Could one of you please go outside so you can flag down the ambulance that's coming as well?'

'Blood pressure eighty over fifty,' Mitch

told her as the reading came up on the life pack. He was rapidly sticking electrodes on Bruce's chest, pulling his unbuttoned shirt aside to attach the final leads that circled the left side of his chest to end under the armpit line.

The blood pressure was far too low. Jenna reached for the IV kit. 'I'm going to put a small line in your arm,' she told her patient. 'Just in case we need to give you some fluids and medication. Is that okay with you?'

'Sure…if you think I need it… Am I having a heart attack or something?'

'That's what we want to find out.'

'Hang in there, Bruce,' an onlooker said. 'You'll be all right.'

'Heaven help the rest of us if he isn't.' The barber was back, holding a stainless-steel bowl. 'He's the healthiest bloke here by a mile. He even ran the London Marathon last year.'

'I did.' Bruce leaned his head back on the seat cushion. 'Feels like a million years ago right now.'

'Do you have any medical conditions we should know about?' Jenna asked. 'Like your blood pressure or anything to do with your heart?'

'Don't like doctors,' Bruce said. 'Haven't been for a year or two.'

'Are you allergic to any medication that you know of?'

'No. Don't like pills, either. Haven't even taken an aspirin that I can remember in recent times.'

Mitch was printing out a piece of paper from the life pack and Jenna bent her head to see what might be revealed by the twelve lead ECG documenting the electrical activity of Bruce's heart.

She expected to see the wide spacing between beats due to the slow rate. She wasn't surprised to see that Mitch's finger was touching the squares that were abnormal in rapid succession, his voice no more than a murmur.

'Look at that PR interval,' he said.

'Mmm. First degree heart block.'

'And here…and here…' He touched the capital W and M shapes showing in the chest leads. 'Left bundle branch block. I wonder if it's new or old?'

Jenna was wondering too. As a new development it could indicate that Bruce was, indeed, suffering a heart attack and it could be a serious one. 'I'll get that IV line in. Could you draw up some atropine?'

'Sure. I'll set up an adrenaline infusion, too, shall I?'

'Please.' Jenna's fleeting glance was the only appreciation she had time to show. How good was it to be working with someone who knew more than she did about how to deal with a situation that could potentially turn to custard at any moment? Someone that she trusted probably more than any crew member she'd ever worked with in the past.

How good was it that it was Friday? Her day—and at least part of her evening—with Mitch? Not that this was the time to allow even a momentary thought about what she knew that would include but her body knew and, somehow, it gave her even more energy and focus for the task at hand. Having Mitch with her out on the road always had this effect—as if it only took his presence to turn up the volume on anything in her life. Work, sharing a meal, conversation…making love…

Today, like most days with Mitch as her crew partner, was flying past and cardiac call-outs seemed to be the theme for this shift. They'd already been to a chest pain with an apparently non-cardiac cause and an episode of angina that wasn't responsive to the elderly woman's normal medication so she had been taken to hospital for further tests. A drug overdose on the back seat of a bus had kept them busy for long enough to create a large traffic jam on a busy road and put them in the right area of the city to be the rapid response for the urgent call from this barber's shop.

'Sharp scratch,' she warned Bruce. She slid the cannula into his vein, blocked the end of it while she screwed a Luer plug into place and then put the clear, sticky covering over the line to protect it, turning to look over her shoulder at the screen of the life pack. Mitch was filling a syringe from an ampoule but he was also watching the screen.

'PR interval's stretching,' he said quietly. 'We're losing the P wave in the T wave.' He taped the ampoule to the syringe barrel and handed it to Jenna. 'Atropine, zero point six milligrams.'

But Bruce's abnormal rhythm wasn't responsive to the first drug. Or to the adrenaline they tried next as an infusion. His rate, in fact, was dropping.

'Rate's in the twenties.' Mitch was supporting Bruce as his level of consciousness dropped to the point where they needed to move him onto the floor. 'Shall we pace him?'

Jenna nodded. Even if the ambulance arrived in the next few seconds, it would be unsafe to transport Bruce to the hospital when his heart rate was now too slow to be life sustaining. External pacing, by delivering electric shocks to stimulate the heart, could be effective but painful. About to ask Mitch to draw up a powerful analgesic, Jenna's heart sank as an alarm on the life pack suddenly sounded.

'He's in VF.' Mitch pushed the button that would charge the defibrillator and the increasing pitch of the new sound was added to the alarm still bleeping.

Bruce's heart was in the process of stopping completely. This had suddenly become a cardiac arrest and the change in the tension of this call-out was all the more dramatic as the ambulance crew arrived, two paramedics and an observer who looked young enough to be a medical student. Due to the medical hierarchy, Mitch automatically had the position of leading this resuscitation but it didn't feel like that to Jenna. They had become so tightly welded as a team over the many weeks they had been doing these shifts together that they could virtually read each other's minds and have equipment ready or drugs drawn up so that the protocol became a seamless performance.

'Stand clear…'

'Clear.' Jenna wriggled back on her knees. She needed to, anyway, to reach the airway kit that was going to be needed to intubate.

'Shocking…'

She could hear the gasp from Bruce's barber shop friends behind her. Some crews would try and clear an area of spectators when something was happening that might not end well but Jenna's opinion was that if they weren't children, they weren't in the way, and they wanted to be there, witnessing that everything possible was being done for someone could make the experience less traumatic.

And it was one of those all too rare occasions when it looked as if the audience was going to witness a successful resuscitation because, with just the first shock of the defibrillator, there seemed to be a rhythm appearing on the screen as the interference from the shock faded. Mitch held up his hand to stop the paramedic about to start chest compressions.

'Wait. Let it settle...'

Yes. They could all see the spikes of a normal, sinus rhythm. Still too slow but enough to keep blood circulating and keep Bruce alive. They definitely needed to get him to hospital as soon as possible, however, and he was going to need very careful monitoring and medication dosages.

Minutes later, they had Bruce on a stretcher and Jenna was happy he was stable enough to move.

'Dr Mitchell and I will come in with you,' she told the ambulance crew. 'Can one of you bring my vehicle, please?'

'I can do that as soon as we're loaded.' One of the paramedics stepped forward to take the keys. He turned to the observer. 'You can come with me. You don't want a crowd in the back of the truck if things need to happen fast.'

Jenna nodded in answer to the unspoken query from the other paramedic. 'Yes, we can load. Mitch, can you stay with him? I need to make a call and find the closest hospital with available, emergency PCI facilities.'

'Is he going to be okay?' The barber wasn't the only person looking pale here now.

'We're going to take the best possible care of him,' Jenna assured them all. 'And we'll be taking him to a hospital that can treat him for whatever's going on.'

The hospital with the ability to deal urgently with a life-threatening blockage of coronary arteries was a little out of Jenna's usual patch for her rapid response vehicle but the longer drive towards Central London gave them enough time to stabilise Bruce's condition and he was regaining consciousness as they handed over to the cardiology team waiting for them. A short time later, as the team prepared to rush him into the catheter laboratory to diagnose and treat any blockages in his coronary arteries, he was awake enough to recognise Jenna and Mitch.

'Thank you,' he said to them, his voice shaky. 'I think I owe you guys one...'

Walking to find where the vehicle had been parked to one side of the ambulance bay, Jenna smiled at Mitch.

'That doesn't happen often, does it?'

'Someone waking up after a cardiac arrest and saying "Thanks"?' Mitch grinned. 'No, it doesn't happen often. That was a great job.'

'Be even better if it's the one we can finish the shift on but I don't like our chances. It's going to take a while to get back to station from here, which means plenty of opportunities to be needed somewhere.'

'I'll have to come back this way later, too, so I hope we don't run late. Dad and Ollie are at the zoo.'

'Oh… I'd completely forgotten you told me about that school trip coming up.' Jenna climbed into the driver's seat. 'Good grief… we've been so busy today I hadn't even asked how the family is. It's been ages since Pets' Day.'

'I don't expect you to remember everything in my family diary,' Mitch said. 'They came in on the train but I've arranged to pick them up. We'll have dinner in town and then I'll take them home.'

So they wouldn't have the couple of hours of private time together that had so quickly become the highlight of Jenna's weeks. That the disappointment was so sharp should be a warning, Jenna thought. Was she getting too dependent on Mitch's friendship? That hadn't been a part of the plan. She would never intentionally become dependent on anything or anyone again. Because that meant trouble if it disappeared and she'd had enough of coping with that kind of adjustment in her life already. So she squashed the disappointment.

She had no claims on Mitch's time. If he was available to be with her, that was great. If he wasn't, that was no big deal and, after all, he was spending his whole day with her. Come to think of it, that had to be a big deal for Mitch, being with her rather than his son.

'You're missing a school trip with Ollie?' Her tone revealed her astonishment. 'To come out on the road with me?'

'Well…apart from how much I love my Fridays with you, there was a limit of how many parent helpers could go. Dad won Rock, Paper, Scissors, so he got the day at the zoo. Actually, I would have let him have the treat, anyway. He deserves it—he does so much for me and Ollie.' Mitch reached for his seatbelt. 'He always has. My life would have fallen apart completely after Tegan died if he hadn't been there for me.'

'He's a lovely man, your dad. I really liked him.'

'He really liked you, too,' Mitch said. 'So

did Ollie. They're both still talking about how excited you got when Jet won the fancy dress competition and Ollie's been asking when he's going to see you again.'

'Has he?' Jenna's heart gave an odd little squeeze at the idea of Ollie remembering her, let alone asking to see her again. Being with Ollie, along with so many other children, on Pets' Day had had its moments of challenge but, overall, it had felt like a positive step in a new direction. Knowing that she had become someone that Ollie was talking about when she wasn't there was disconcerting, however, and Jenna wasn't sure if that squeezing sensation was pleasant or not. It felt like it could go either way if it got any stronger so it might be a good idea to change the subject.

'Was your mother around as well?' she queried.

'No. She died when I was fourteen so it was just me and Dad after that.' Mitch let his breath out in a sigh. 'They say history doesn't repeat itself but it kind of felt like that when I went back home with my motherless baby and it was me and Dad running the show.'

'You were lucky to have the support. My

family—and Stefan's—were thin on the ground and living too far away.'

'I'll bet you coped brilliantly,' Mitch told her.

'I had good friends.' Jenna nodded. She caught his gaze. 'Friends are gold, aren't they?' Maybe she wanted to reassure him that it wasn't a big deal that they couldn't be together this evening. That this was a friendship that wasn't held together only by a sexual connection. 'Especially the ones who step up in the bad times,' she added, remembering her close friends that had been there for her when Stefan—and then Eli— had died. 'The ones who are there for you, no matter what.'

Mitch was holding her gaze. 'I'll be there for you, Jenna,' he said softly. 'Anytime. Don't ever forget that, will you?'

Oh, man…that squeezy feeling around her heart had suddenly made it impossible to take a new breath. This was it, wasn't it? The thing that had been missing from her life. It hadn't been simply about the lack of physical touch and closeness, it was this—having someone who cared enough to make a commitment to be there. To share even a part of her life for the foreseeable future and then some. Jenna remembered that moment in the motorway service area when she'd been watching that young couple and their children and she'd compared Mitch to Stefan.

She'd thought the light had gone out of her world when she'd lost Stefan and that Mitch was quieter and more mature and…maybe less exciting? But he had brought a different kind of light into her life, hadn't he? Maybe not fireworks, but a steady, comforting light that gave warmth as well. She had to close her eyes for a heartbeat with that realisation and find that new breath because it felt, absurdly, as if she wanted to cry. And Mitch had obviously noticed.

'Tired?'

'I wouldn't say "no" to a coffee, that's for sure.' Jenna made sure her tone was upbeat. 'Have we even had a break since our lunch got cut to less than ten minutes?'

'Don't think so.'

Jenna picked up the radio handset and called in their availability. She also told her friend, Adam, in the control centre that she was suffering from caffeine withdrawal. He laughed.

'No promises, Jenna, but go and get your

coffee fix. I'll keep you on standby as long
as possible.'

There was a coffee shop well positioned
to take advantage of hospital staff patronage
so it was only minutes until they were sitting
back in their vehicle with paper cups of delicious coffee and some homemade blueberry
muffins. Even if this break only lasted a few
minutes, she was going to make the most of
it. The warmth of Mitch confirming how
important their friendship was had added
yet another layer to the connection they'd
forged since they'd first met each other and
that was helping to make up for any disappointment about this evening.

'So you're going to go and pick up your
dad and Ollie straight after our shift?' Jenna
managed to sound perfectly cheerful as she
spoke around a mouthful of muffin. 'Is that
early enough? If we get back to station soon,
I'm happy to take any last call solo. What
time does the zoo visit end?'

'The others are all heading back to the
train station at four p.m.' Mitch looked at
his watch. 'So that's only half an hour away,
but Dad said he and Ollie would go and get
an ice cream somewhere and wait for me.
Or they might go and feed the squirrels in

Regent's Park. It's no problem. We haven't booked anywhere special for dinner, we're just going to find a place we like the look of.'

And then Mitch would be driving his family home. Away from London. Away from her. Okay…maybe that disappointment hadn't been entirely made up for. It was normally easy not to even think about being in bed with Mitch while they were on duty, or even having a bit of a break from being on active duty like they were at the moment, but right now, it was filling Jenna's mind and the pull towards touching Mitch became suddenly overwhelming so it was just as well she had her hands full of coffee and muffin. They shouldn't even touch, let alone kiss each other when they were in the rapid response vehicle but there was nothing to stop them sharing a glance.

A long glance that could say such a lot. Mitch could let her know that he was going to miss their time together later just as much as she was. Then he cleared his throat.

'What would you say if I suggested we went away sometime? Just for a weekend break. Somewhere…nice…'

Somewhere nice? Was that a euphemism for somewhere 'romantic'? Jenna took a slow sip of her coffee as she thought about that. Would she want it to be? Judging from the way her heart rate suddenly picked up, the answer to that question seemed to be affirmative.

'You mean, like Paris?'

Mitch made a face. 'Maybe not Paris. I proposed to Tegan there, on top of the Eiffel tower. How 'bout… Barcelona?'

Jenna shook her head. 'Stefan and I went there on our Spanish honeymoon.'

The wry smile they shared was acknowledging more than crossing potential weekend destinations off a shortlist. It was also about understanding how important the memories were of the people they'd loved enough to marry. That they would always be a part of their lives and…maybe that, because this was a friendship with no expectations on either side, it wasn't a threat to those memories. They didn't have to feel disloyal. Maybe, Jenna needed to dismiss that idea about time away being romantic so she didn't undermine that trust.

She dropped the rest of her muffin into her empty coffee cup. She started the engine but didn't immediately pick up the radio microphone to call in their availability. She didn't pull out into the traffic, either. She felt like she was holding her breath to hear what Mitch was going to say next.

'I think we need to find somewhere just for us. Somewhere neither of us has ever been.' Mitch finished his coffee. 'Can't be too far away, though. I'm quite confident that Ollie and Dad would be delighted to have their first weekend alone together but that wouldn't give us enough time to get to the Antarctic. Or the middle of Africa.'

'I've always wanted to go to one of the Greek islands,' Jenna said. 'Like Mykonos. The pictures always make it look like paradise. White buildings and blue, blue sea and sky, fishing boats and pelicans and a taverna right on the beach.'

Oh… Dear Lord, how romantic would *that* be? And why wasn't that thought being shut down as quickly and completely as she knew it should be?

'Let's do it,' Mitch said softly. 'Just for a day or two. Just us…'

And there they were again, looking at each other and saying things silently and… the pull was irresistible. Jenna had to lean closer and it seemed like the magnetism was working on both sides because Mitch leaned towards her at exactly the same time. It wasn't a real kiss—that would have been utterly unprofessional—but the brief butterfly brush of their lips was just as powerful.

It reminded Jenna of their very first kiss in her kitchen that evening, after Mitch's FRAME course had finished. For ever ago. If she'd known that she would be sitting here a few months later with butterflies of excitement in her belly at the thought of a romantic weekend away with Mitch, she would have run as far and as fast as possible away from him that night. How on earth had the idea of their friendship growing into something more not only become acceptable but something she actually wanted?

She remembered this kind of feeling. Those butterfly tendrils of sensation that were excitement and yearning and desire all tumbling together.

It was the feeling of falling in love, that's what it was.

And even that realisation wasn't enough to scare her as much as she might have expected. Because part of her wanted to fall in love. To feel that astonishing kind of magic again. She had to turn away swiftly enough that Mitch didn't see even a hint of that flash of thoughts. It wasn't as if she was sure about it herself, anyway. And it certainly wasn't part of their agreement. If Mitch knew, it might spell the end of their friendship and Jenna didn't want that to happen. She *really* didn't want that to happen. And yet, in that nanosecond before she'd broken the gaze they were sharing after that almost kiss, she could almost swear that she could see a reflection of her own thoughts in Mitch's eyes.

And that thought was too much to take in just yet. Reaching for the radio microphone, Jenna turned up the volume of background radio transmissions as well, as if it could distract them both from whatever disconcerting potential change in their friendship that might be happening.

Not that Mitch was showing any signs of being disconcerted. Or scared off.

'It sounds like a plan,' he said. 'I reckon we both deserve a bit of a break and how nice would it be to sit on a beach and soak up some sun? Let's talk about it again next Friday. In the meantime, why don't you come with us tonight? For dinner?'

'I can't crash your special family dinner.'

The beeping from the radio was a city ambulance responding to a call.

'Roger that. ETA five minutes for London Zoo.'

The mention of the zoo did more than catch the attention of both Mitch and Jenna. She reached to turn up the volume even more. Mitch froze.

Beep... Beep... 'Any further patient details?'

'Coming through on your pagers. Sixty-eight-year-old man with severe chest pain and shortness of breath. He's just inside the front gates.'

Mitch had gone pale. 'Dad's sixty-eight,' he said.

Jenna pushed the 'talk' button on the side of her microphone. By chance, she was connected to Adam again.

'Rapid Response One available. I'd like to respond to that cardiac call to London Zoo as back-up. My crew partner's father is there at the moment. Same age.'

'Understood,' Adam said briskly. 'Logging you in.'

The call came through on their radio only seconds later. 'Control to Rapid Response One. Code Blue, please, to London Zoo. Chest pain.'

'Rapid Response One to Control. Roger that. On our way.' Jenna hit the switch to

start the beacons flashing on the roof. She
also activated the siren. She kept her gaze
firmly on the heavy traffic around them as
she pushed her way through. She didn't want
to look at Mitch because she knew she'd see
the fear in his eyes.

It was not just a day for a run of cardiac
calls.

It was, apparently, a day for feelings that
Jenna hadn't experienced in a very long
time. A rollercoaster of emotions, in fact.

The warmth of feeling that close connection to someone.

Disappointment that they wouldn't get that
special time together.

The flicker of the kind of intensity that
only came from falling in love.

And…now the fear. Of the kind of loss
that only came from losing a loved one.

Jenna didn't want Mitch to have to go
through that again. Surely life could never
be that unfair?

She pushed her foot down on the accelerator as they hit a clearer stretch of road. She
knew only too well that there were no guar-
antees of life ever being fair. She also knew
that there was only one reason why she was
feeling this so intensely.

It was because she cared so much about how this might affect Mitch.

Because she cared so much about *him*.

This was love. Maybe not the bells and whistles that went with the 'falling in love' process and all the romantic gestures but this was real.

As real as it got…

CHAPTER NINE

'IT'S NOTHING. I don't know why everyone's making such a fuss.'

'Chest pain is never something to ignore, Mr Mitchell.'

The senior ambulance paramedic was sticking ECG electrodes in place on Mitch's father's chest as he and Jenna stood to one side, having arrived a minute or two later than the ambulance crew. He still looked pale, Jenna thought, and Ollie, who was in his father's arms, looked even more worried. His dark eyes looked enormous in that small, pale face and he had a flop of soft hair hanging over his forehead that made her want to reach out and smooth it back before it got too close to his eyes. She didn't, however. She, like Mitch, was waiting anxiously to see what might be revealed on the twelve lead ECG that was about to be recorded.

'Call me Mike. Please.'

'Sure. Do you have any other problems with your health that we should know about, Mike?'

'*Other* problems? You mean a bit of indigestion isn't enough?' Michael Mitchell's wry smile faded as he realised his attempt at humour had fallen flat. He shook his head. 'My GP, here, can tell you anything you want to know.'

'He's treated for high cholesterol and hypertension,' Mitch said. 'Blood pressure's well controlled, though…' He glanced at the reading on the life pack beside where the lines of the ECG were showing. 'It's a bit higher than usual at the moment.'

Jenna could hear the layer of anxiety beneath the calm words. Never mind brushing Ollie's hair out of his eyes. She found herself shifting a little closer to Mitch and had to fight the urge to touch his hand with her own. To let her fingers curl around his in the hope of offering support. To let him know he wasn't alone.

'Are you surprised?' His father asked, irritably. 'I didn't want anybody calling an ambulance. I'm wasting everybody's time. If I hadn't told the teachers to get going, the whole school would have missed their train back to Allensbury.'

'You're not wasting anybody's time,' the paramedic assured him. 'We'd much rather get called and find there's nothing wrong than not be called when there is.'

But Michael didn't seem to be listening. He made a sound that could have been a stifled groan and rubbed at the centre of his chest.

'How bad is that pain, sir?' the paramedic asked. 'On a scale of zero to ten with zero being no pain and ten the worst you can imagine?'

Michael shrugged. 'About a four.'

'Translate that as being at least six,' Mitch said. 'He's not one to complain about anything. I'd make it an eight, actually, judging by how green around the gills he's looking. Is the pain just in the centre of your chest, Dad?'

'Where's he green?' Ollie asked. His question was a frightened whisper but Jenna could hear it as clearly as if he was in her own arms, rather than Mitch's. 'I can't see...'

'It's just an expression, sweetheart,' Jenna whispered, seeing that Mitch's attention was firmly on his father. 'He's not *really* green.'

'It does kind of go through to my back,' Michael admitted.

'What's the matter with Grandpa?' Ollie sounded on the verge of tears now.

Mitch shifted Ollie in his arms so that they could see each other's faces. 'Grandpa's not feeling well,' he said gently. 'He's got a sore bit. Like that sore tummy you had a while ago, remember?'

Ollie nodded. 'I was sick. And then I felt better. You said I had a bug. A round bug.'

Jenna found herself smiling. 'A "round" bug? How did Daddy know what shape it was?'

Mitch caught her gaze and she could see a gleam of amusement amidst the anxiety. 'I suspect I said that Ollie had a bug that was going around.'

Ollie nodded again. 'Maybe Grandpa has a round bug, too.'

'It's just a bit of indigestion, lovey,' Michael told him. 'I expect I ate too many of those bacon sarnies for lunch.'

Both Jenna and Mitch stepped closer to the paramedics as the ECG trace was printed.

'Can't see too much to worry about there,' the paramedic said.

'No.' Mitch caught Jenna's gaze as if her opinion mattered as well. She liked that. It was like when they worked together as a team and he always made her feel like an equal partner.

'How's the pain?' she asked Michael.

'Getting better by the minute,' he told her. But when he moved, his face made it very obvious that he was playing it down.

'We'll give you something for that pain.' The paramedic reached for his kit. 'And then we'll take you into hospital so they can find out what's going on.'

Michael looked horrified. 'No. I'm fine. I can go home with my son.'

'Just cooperate, Dad.' Mitch's tone was patient. 'We need to know what's going on. They'll run a few tests and rule out anything we need to worry about.'

He still had Ollie clinging to his neck and maybe Michael could see how frightened his grandson was.

'I'll go—but only if you and Ollie go and have that dinner we were planning. I'm not going to spoil a special day out by having you hanging around a hospital for hours. You can come and pick me up later.'

'Don't be daft. Of course we're coming with you.'

'That's not fair on Ollie. He's worried enough as it is, without seeing everything that goes on in an emergency department.'

Jenna could sense a standoff happening. She could also sense that, underneath his bravado, Michael was probably as worried about his own health as his family was. She could see how tense Mitch was and…as for Ollie, well…her heart just went out to the scared little boy.

'I could look after Ollie,' she offered. 'My shift's about to finish and the vehicle's not needed back on station any time soon.'

The swift glance from Mitch told Jenna that he didn't want her doing anything she might not be comfortable with. That he knew how big a deal this was.

'You don't have to do that,' he said quietly. 'We'll be fine.'

'I know I don't.'

And even yesterday, maybe she wouldn't have made that offer, even though she had chosen to meet Ollie and attend Pets' Day because it was a big step to changing her life for the better. This was something else. Another huge shift and it was happening because of how she was feeling about Mitch. This was about finding out whether she could cope with being with Ollie as a parent figure, because, if she couldn't, there was no point in dreaming about falling in love with Andrew Mitchell or of them having any kind of future together. And the part of her that was longing for that seemed to be growing.

Jenna found a smile. 'I wouldn't have offered if I didn't want to. We'll stay within easy reach of the hospital. You'll be able to text whenever you want me to bring Ollie back.'

His glance was asking silently if she really thought she could cope. By way of responding, she turned to Michael. 'Will you go and have those tests done, Mike, if I'm looking after Ollie? So that everyone can stop worrying about you?'

'If it's really okay with you, Jenna.'

Jenna still didn't meet Mitch's gaze. 'That's settled then,' she said brightly. Ollie? Do you want to come with me in my car or ride in the ambulance with Daddy and Grandpa to the hospital?'

'I want to go in the ambulance.' Ollie's eyes were wide. 'Can I do the siren?'

'We'll see about that.' The paramedics

shared a glance. And a smile. 'Maybe just a blip when we get outside the gates. We don't want to scare the animals, do we?'

'So...what would you like to do first?'

Ollie was still staring through the automatic glass doors that led from the ambulance loading bay into the emergency department of the same hospital Mitch and Jenna had brought their last patient to, even though the stretcher carrying his grandfather had now disappeared from view. His father had also disappeared from view and Jenna knew that this little boy had to be feeling lost. When his small hand crept into hers she froze just for a heartbeat because it was the first time since Eli that she had held the hand of a child that wasn't a patient.

She took a quick, inward breath. She'd told Mitch she could cope. And she could. This was a step she wanted to take, she reminded herself. Like Pets' Day, this was a step towards a better future. A life that she could live to the fullest. With both Mitch and his son, if he ever felt the same way.

She gave Ollie's hand a gentle squeeze. 'Are you hungry?'

A small face tilted up towards her. A small head nodded.

'What do you like to eat? More than anything else?'

'Hamburgers.' Had Ollie noticed the group of shops across the road that included many of the most popular fast food outlets? 'And chips. The ones that come with a toy.'

Jenna grinned. She knew exactly which child-friendly chain he was talking about. 'Are you allowed to eat hamburgers and chips?' Maybe she needed to text Mitch and check.

'Only sometimes,' Ollie admitted.

Jenna didn't want to disturb Mitch unless it was for something important. She knew that blood samples would be being taken as part of the examination his father needed. And another ECG. Maybe a scan or X-rays as well. There was still the concern that it could be a cardiac pain and it had just been too early in the process for the ECG changes to have shown up at the zoo.

'I think this is definitely a "sometimes",' she told Ollie. 'There's a playground in there, too, isn't there? Look… I can see the big pipe that comes out the side of the building from here. Is that a slide?'

'You climb in it.' Ollie's grip on her hand tightened as they started walking away from the hospital. 'I can show you, if you like.'

It felt like he was offering Jenna his trust in that handhold. As if, just for the moment, she was the person that mattered the most in his world. That was a reminder of just how big this step she was taking was, but it was actually easier to take a new breath this time.

'I'd like that very much,' she said.

They both ate hamburgers and French fries. Ollie was thrilled with the toy car that came with his meal and drove it round the table between the hamburger boxes and along a road he made out of leftover fries. When he realised he was making engine noises he glanced up at Jenna, as if he was worried he was being too noisy, but when she smiled his face lit up and he went back to driving the little blue car.

Jenna was perfectly happy to sit and watch. She needed the time to take this in. To let herself be in the moment and know that this was Ollie, not Eli. That this was about the future and not the past. That it was okay to have a part of her heart that ached but it was also okay to have a part that could find joy in a small boy's happiness.

Ollie wanted Jenna to watch him try out everything the playground had to offer after that. He waved at her from the windows in the climbing pipes, bounced on seats set on huge springs, played in the pit full of brightly coloured balls and finally came back to where Jenna was sitting.

'Will you read me a story?' he begged. 'In the quiet corner?'

'Of course.'

It was the perfect way to fill in the rest of the time that she needed to care for Ollie. Having let Mitch know where they were and that Ollie was happy, he had texted back to say that his father had been cleared of any cardiac issues and that the diagnosis for his chest pain was likely to be a severe dose of gastric reflux. They were waiting at the pharmacy to pick up some medication and then Mitch would order a taxi for the three of them to get back to his car and they would come and collect Ollie when it arrived.

Ollie curled up in the soft cushion of one of the oversized bean bags near the book-shelves and leaned his head against Jenna's shoulder as she read. He still had the little blue car clutched in his hand and he was clearly worn out from all the playing because she could feel his head getting heavier and his body softening against her arm. And… she could smell a faint whiff of, what was it? Oh…yes…*baby shampoo*…

Her voice faltered as she tried to keep reading and then trailed into silence but it didn't matter because Ollie was too sleepy to notice. And Jenna had a whole new idea to grapple with—the knowledge that it would be just as easy to fall in love with this child as with his father. That maybe she was a lot closer to that point than she realised. The thought was too big to allow herself to go there and Jenna could almost feel mental doors slamming shut in an effort to protect her from the fear that was hovering. Waiting to step in and force her to flee.

So she simply sat there without moving a muscle. Letting Ollie sleep. Holding herself together until she could find a new level of calmness. This wouldn't last long. Mitch would be here any minute to collect his son and then she could get herself home to her safe space and maybe then she could step back far enough to think about this new shift in her thinking.

Seeing Mitch coming through the restaurant area made her even more confident that

she was coping with this. Seeing the smile
on his face as he saw Ollie asleep beside her
was enough to make her feel very proud of
how she was coping. Shifting to give Mitch
room to scoop Ollie up was enough to wake
the little boy but he wasn't upset by the interruption. He sat up and blinked and then
smiled happily, first at Jenna and then at his
father.

'I'm the same as Mia now, aren't I?' he
said.

'Are you?' Mitch raised his eyebrows as
he shared a glance with Jenna.

Ollie nodded. 'She always has her mummy
to watch her playing. Now I've got one, too.'

Again, Mitch glanced at Jenna but she
dodged the eye contact. Her mouth had just
gone very dry. This had gone way too far.
Way too fast. She couldn't keep those doors
shut any longer and she could feel panic closing in on her. She couldn't do this, after all.
The enormity of those emotions and that fear
that came with them was too much.

The last straw was Ollie starting to climb
out of the squashy bean chair and losing his
balance. Or maybe he was just wanting a
cuddle. Whatever the reason, the thought
of having those small arms winding them-

selves around her neck was instantly unbearable. Without even thinking about it, Jenna pushed him away, scrambling to her feet as she blindly reacted to the instinct to run. Ollie tried to hold on, fell back into the chair and then rolled off to land with a bump on the floor, whereupon he burst into tears.

Jenna froze, appalled at what had just happened. She could feel that Mitch was just as horrified, although he calmly stepped forward to lift Ollie into his arms.

'Come on, buddy. You're okay...'

'I'm sorry...' Jenna bit her lip. 'I didn't mean... I...'

What was she trying to say? That she hadn't done it on purpose? Surely Mitch couldn't possibly think that was the case anyway?

But there was an edge of anger in the steady gaze Mitch was giving her over the head of a still sobbing Ollie.

'I get it,' he said slowly. 'But I'm not about to let my son get hurt by it. You said you could cope...'

There was something else that was being said silently, as well.

How could you?

'I'm sorry...' she said again.

'Yeah… I know. Me, too.' Mitch was turning away. 'It's time I got Ollie and Dad home. 'Bye, Jenna.'

The farewell had a chilly edge that generated a new fear in Jenna. 'You'll be back next week?' It was a plea as much as a question. 'For our shift?'

Mitch turned his head. 'I don't think that's a very good idea,' he said slowly. 'For any of us. Do you?'

Jenna didn't say anything. She didn't move as she watched Mitch carry his son out of the restaurant. Away from her. She ducked her head as she fought back tears and it was then that she noticed the little blue car lying on the floor. Without thinking, she stooped and picked it up. She could feel the sharp edges of the toy cutting into her hand as she walked out herself but she welcomed the physical discomfort.

It was so much easier to handle than the emotional pain she knew was waiting for her.

CHAPTER TEN

IT SHOULD HAVE worn off by now.

This horrible, empty feeling.

Missing Mitch so much it was an actual physical pain that was, predictably, there at times like being alone in her bed in those wakeful hours in the dead of the night but could also sideswipe her at unexpected times, like now—when Jenna was sitting up late to check the content of tomorrow's planned teaching sessions.

She needed to simplify the session on ophthalmic emergencies. That quiz of medical terminology might be fun for a group of highly trained doctors but it was very likely to be obscure for the paramedics and nurses that were here to so the five day introductory FRAME course. Throwing in one or two, for interest's sake, like diplopia and ecchymosis, was fine but even amongst experienced doctors, Mitch had been a standout in knowing that enophthalmos was the displacement of an eyeball.

It was suddenly so much harder to focus on the Day Three programme she was checking as Jenna fought off yet another wave of that pain. For heaven's sake…how long was it going to take? It had been weeks now.

'Stick to the basics,' she muttered aloud, as she deleted a slide of the presentation and added a different one. 'Recognition and initial management of the most common eye injuries. There we go…corneal abrasions, foreign bodies, chemical injuries, blunt trauma…'

She had to focus on making this course the best it could possibly be because it was special. Jenna was in Northern Ireland for the first time, as the FRAME initiative was expanded yet again and the interest from medics wanting to do the course and the wider public was huge. A film crew had sat in on a session or two on the first day and had interviewed the course participants. Clips of Jenna teaching and her class revealing what an exciting addition to their practices this qualification would be had been shown as part of her appearance on breakfast television early this morning to explain the reason the FRAME initiative had been developed in the first place and the measurable difference it had made to the outcomes in medical emergencies in rural areas.

Not that Jenna had explained that the main reason FRAME had been developed had been her desperate need for a new direction in her career that could give her a purpose in life during those dreadful, empty months after she'd lost her precious son. Or that throwing herself, heart and soul, into the formation and delivery of the initiative had become her entire life. That it was now in every part of the United Kingdom was something to be very proud of and being here, in Belfast, taking the very first course should have been the absolute highlight of her career so far.

And it was. Of course it was. Jenna was immensely proud of what she'd achieved since she'd started this journey but...but it didn't come close to filling that empty space in her life.

That wave of missing Mitch hadn't completely worn off and the thought of lying awake yet again tonight after such an early start and a long day since was so unappealing that Jenna did something she never normally did when she was travelling for work. She went to the mini bar in her room and took out one of the half-sized bottles of wine. Just a glass, she promised herself, because it might help her to sleep, if nothing else.

For the minute or two it took to open the bottle and pour herself the glass of wine, she had to do without the distraction that working on her session content or catching up on emails could have provided and Jenna was too tired to resist the direction her mind was determined to take her.

Back to that course when Mitch had fallen into her life. Back to that moment when she been captured by this man. Not by something as shallow as his physical appearance but by that aura of being able to take command of any space or situation he was in. By the impression that he was searching for something of significance and that perhaps she was the person who could help him find what he was looking for.

Most of all, by him being the first man she had been attracted to since Stefan.

Jenna unscrewed the lid of the bottle and opened a cupboard to find a glass. The way she was feeling now was her own fault, she reminded herself. She was the one who'd talked herself into following through on that attraction. Had she really been naïve enough to believe that it was simply an experiment that would not necessarily have any negative impact on her life? She'd recognised that there was a gap in her life, no matter how satisfying her career was, and the experiment was to find out whether the addition of a physical connection with another human could fill at least part of the void she'd learned to live with and have the opposite of a negative impact.

And it had. It had filled it to the point of overflowing. To the point where Jenna had not only not wanted it to end but she'd wanted more. A lifetime of more, preferably. And now she had to try and learn to live with the flipside of that kind of connection—the loss and loneliness of finding herself right back in that empty space.

Jenna poured the wine into the tumbler she'd taken from the cupboard. She hadn't heard from Mitch since that awful day when he'd walked out of her life with his crying son in his arms. She'd hurt Ollie and she could understand that he would not permit that to happen again. She would have been just as protective of Eli so she could also understand that another apology from her would make no difference.

If he'd chosen to see her again as something that had no connection to his personal life—or even just come out for a shift with her again—she would have believed that things could have been fixed but he hadn't made contact. He didn't want anything to do with her any longer so there was nothing she could do about that empty space other than to learn to live with it. To try and find her way to leave it behind far enough to fence it off. She needed to try and find those protective filters that she used to view life through, which had somehow been lost during her time with Mitch.

Having been through coping with loss before didn't make it any easier, though. The void felt bigger, if anything and, in moments like this, Jenna felt as if she was actually falling into it and would become instantly and heartbreakingly lost.

It was so empty.

So lonely.

The experiment had backfired. Jenna had found exactly what was missing from her life and it wasn't anything as simple as sex.

It was love.

It was that feeling of family.

Oh…help… Tears were imminent now. Jenna picked up the glass and took a large mouthful of the wine. She felt her face crumpling as it hit her taste buds, however, and seconds later, she was leaning over the basin in the bathroom, to spit the wine out. Even then, she needed a mouthful of water to try and get the incredibly sour taste from her mouth. Despite being a wine she'd had and enjoyed in the past, this particular bottle was horrendous.

Corked?

No. It had a screw top.

Maybe she was coming down with something?

A 'round' bug, perhaps?

Jenna felt a tear escape and roll down the side of her nose at that memory of Ollie and then something shifted into place at the back of her mind. A memory of the only other time she'd ever found a mouthful of wine so revolting she'd had to spit it out before it made her sick. She could almost hear Stefan laughing at her and what he'd said afterwards.

I bet you're pregnant... Let's do a test...

No…

No, no, no. It couldn't possibly be why the wine tasted so bad. She and Mitch had taken precautions. It wasn't even as if she was late with her period but, just to double-check, Jenna went to her diary and began counting the days. When she went past twenty-eight days, she felt a cold trickle of fear down her spine.

She was never late.

Ever.

But she was this time. Her period should have started at least two days ago and she didn't even have a hint of the cramps that always came as a warning. Stunned, Jenna sat unmoving. She couldn't even begin to imagine what this could mean in her life. If she could have chosen one thing that she never wanted to happen ever again, it was this.

Being pregnant.

Knowing that one day, in the not too distant future, she would be holding another baby in her arms.

She couldn't do it.

But she couldn't *not* do it, either.

It was almost funny, in retrospect, to have thought that a glass of wine might help her sleep but Jenna's huff of laughter wasn't amused. It felt rather more like despair.

* * *

His patient was only in her early sixties but it was clear that she was suffering a potentially catastrophic neurological event—a stroke or an aneurysm perhaps. Shona Barry was well known at the Allensbury Surgery due to her frequent visits to manage the kind of problems that came with a lifelong struggle with obesity, like high blood pressure, diabetes, respiratory and cardiac issues. The main problem right now, however, was that Shona's weight was going to present a huge challenge for Mitch to intubate her to secure her airway.

A helicopter had been dispatched from a London hospital that had a dedicated emergency unit for stroke patients but it was still ten minutes away. Mitch had been paged as the local FRAME doctor and had arrived at the same time as their local ambulance service to face dealing with precisely the kind of case that had prompted him to go to that course in the first place.

Having to deal with a difficult airway.

He had positioned Shona's head and one of the two paramedics was pre-oxygenating her, the other was drawing up the drugs needed. Mitch had a cricothyroidotomy kit unrolled as an insurance policy because he knew that this was likely to be a difficult intubation and if he wasn't successful within the maximum three attempts, he would move swiftly on to creating a surgical airway. He also had his video laryngoscope and the stylet to help shape the endotracheal tube as it was manoeuvred past the vocal cords.

As focused as he was on his task, Mitch was also aware of something that wasn't even here.

Jenna.

Part of his brain was back in that classroom, using this equipment with a mannequin. He could sense the same anxiety of failure but he could also feel the confidence that Jenna had exuded. That belief that he was going to succeed. He could actually hear an echo of the calm advice she had given him, regarding the shape of this stylet, when he'd found it difficult to advance the breathing tube through the vocal cords and into the trachea.

Try popping the stylet off with your thumb, back it out a bit and then try advancing the tube...

And, just like it had with that mannequin, the action made it possible to slip the tube into place, check its position and secure it and then move on to everything else that was urgently needed to stabilise Shona's condition before transport to hospital. One of the flight medics took in the challenging size of their patient and the successful intubation and nodded at Mitch.

'Good job,' he murmured. 'I'm sure that wasn't an easy one.'

News that Shona had undergone emergency thrombectomy to remove the clot in a cerebral artery and that she was expected to make a good recovery made that call-out all the more satisfying. The only downside of that interruption to his normal clinic, other than running late for the rest of the day, was that Mitch hadn't been able to shake off that awareness of Jenna. She was just there, in the back of his mind, along with that now familiar ache of missing her.

Getting home was usually enough to be able to shake it off because he had the reason why he'd had to walk away from her right in front of him. Ollie. Mitch would always do whatever he needed to do in order to protect his precious son. Even if it meant giving up a woman he'd fallen in love with. An amazing woman that he was missing with every breath he took, even weeks after that unfortunate incident in the playground of that fast food restaurant.

He'd expected the ache to have faded by now because it had been weeks but today had let him know that it might take a lot longer than expected. Still, he would cope. It was definitely better than that first week, when he'd been so upset by Ollie being so blatantly rejected, worried about his father's health and fighting the urge to contact Jenna when he knew he shouldn't. He had to put Ollie first. He'd vowed to do that when he'd been sitting beside his dying wife.

'I'm going to take such good care of our son,' he'd whispered. *'I'll keep him safe. As healthy and happy as it's possible to be and...and I'll love him with all my heart. I'll never let anything get in the way of that...'*

Ollie was healthy, thank goodness. And happy. Mitch could hear his giggles as he played with Jet in the garden when he arrived home that evening.

'Heard about Shona,' Michael Mitchell said, when Mitch arrived home. He was tossing a salad and there were salmon steaks on the kitchen bench waiting to be grilled.

'Makes you think, doesn't it? You never know what's just around the corner. Could have been me, if that chest pain had been a real heart attack.'

'You're going the right way about improving the chances it won't happen for real.' His father had lost a bit of weight since that scare with the chest pain, modified his diet and was taking some medication. 'That's a nice healthy looking dinner you're making.' Mitch went to the fridge. 'Fancy a beer?'

'Good idea. I imagine it's been a long day for you.'

'Mmm…' Mitch pulled out two bottles of lager. 'It has.' And it wasn't over yet. The feel of those icy bottles in his hands had just triggered a memory of that night in the pub with Jenna. That pleasant surprise of finding that her choice of beverage was just that bit different. The amusement that had danced in her eyes when he'd said that he'd have what she was having. It inevitably morphed into a memory of what had come later that evening when they'd made love that first time and the fresh awareness of what was missing from his life was more than an ache—it was an actual pain.

He stared through the window as he swallowed a mouthful of beer. 'Ollie looks happy.'

'Hmm.' Michael was looking at Mitch rather than his grandson. 'Wish I could say the same about you.'

'I'm fine, Dad.'

'You don't look it. You haven't looked happy for weeks, son. Ever since that visit I had to hospital. You not worried about *my* health, are you?'

Mitch shook his head. 'You're looking better than you have in a long time.'

'So why are you hanging around home so much, then? You loved your days being out in that rapid response vehicle.'

Mitch shrugged. 'I only did that to get back up to speed with the kind of skills I might need in emergencies here.'

'Oh…' His father turned away to get on with his dinner preparations. 'That'll be why you invited Jenna to Pets' Day, then, I guess? Why you've looked happier in the last couple of months than you've been ever since Tegan died.'

Mitch was silent.

'I'm not stupid,' Michael added quietly.

'I know that.' Mitch took another mouthful of his beer. He knew his friendship with

Jenna had made enough of a difference in his life that it was no surprise others had noticed.

'You might be, though.'

'What?'

'If you let Jenna disappear from your life like this.'

'Ollie comes first,' Mitch said. 'And Jenna rejected him. End of.'

Ollie had come through the kitchen door as Mitch was speaking. 'What's "'jected"?' he asked.

'Rejected.' Mitch ruffled his son's soft hair. 'It means that you don't want to accept something that someone's trying to give you. Like a cuddle, maybe. That's what I was talking to Grandpa about—that Jenna didn't want your cuddle.'

Ollie's shrug was so like one of his own gestures that it made Mitch smile.

'Sometimes I 'ject cuddles,' he said. 'If I'm cross. Or sad. You have to be ready for cuddles.' He was heading for the pantry. 'Jenna was sad. Can I have a biscuit, Grandpa?'

'Nope. We're going to have dinner very soon. You can have a bit of carrot, though. Here...' Michael held out a strip of the carrots he was cutting but his gaze was on Mitch.

'Out of the mouths of babes,' he murmured. 'He's not stupid, either.'

But Mitch was frowning. Had he missed something important? That looking after Ollie had made Jenna sad, perhaps? How much worse had he made it, if that was the case, by accusing her of deliberately hurting his son? By not accepting her apology? Not even trying to make contact with her?

Ollie was feeding the carrot stick to Jet. 'Let's go outside again,' he said to the dog. 'And find sticks to throw.'

'Hang on,' Mitch called. 'If it was okay that Jenna didn't want your cuddle, why were you crying so much?'

Ollie didn't bother turning around. 'I lost my car,' he called over his shoulder. 'The blue one that Jenna gave me. And I was sad because it was my favouritest.'

Mitch turned to find himself under his father's steady gaze. 'Maybe Jenna knows where it is,' he said. 'You never know, it might be worth asking.'

Oh…the thought of talking to Jenna. Hearing her voice again gave Mitch an odd feeling in his chest. A tightness that made it noticeably hard to pull in his next breath. He didn't want the concern he could see in his father's eyes though because the thought that his father still felt the same way about him as he did about Ollie was enough to give him a prickle of tears at the back of his eyes. So he turned away, lifting his shoulders in a half-hearted shrug.

'Maybe…'

Jenna had learned how incredibly long a day could seem many years ago. Back when she had been trying to take life one day at a time. Again and again, she'd told herself she only had to get through this one day in order to survive but it felt like it went on for ever.

This had been longer than any of those days.

She wasn't about to try and unpick the emotional threads that were contributing to the crushing weight she was carrying because that would have meant thinking about a future she wouldn't have chosen again in a million years. Another child. Years and years and years of that fear that something terrible could happen and she would have to face the kind of devastation you surely couldn't survive more than once.

It was much better to have something else to focus on and Jenna put everything she had into making the sessions for her class today as memorable as possible as she covered spinal and head injuries, blunt trauma and management of burns. To keep herself busy throughout the evening, Jenna decided to revamp her entire folder of triage scenarios, spending many hours making new cards that listed the injuries and condition of a good variety of patients that could be attached to the mannequins she would arrange tomorrow to look as though they'd been in a bus crash, an explosion or under a collapsed building in an earthquake. Her course attendees would arrive on scene and have to prioritise the patients in order from those who needed immediate, life-saving resuscitation through to those who were so badly injured they were unlikely to survive despite major intervention.

It was a case of rinse or repeat to get through the second to last day of the course where she covered the session on triage along with fracture management, soft tissue injuries and safety around helicopters. It was ironic that the last session of the day was about critical incident stress management when she noticed she had some of the physical symptoms of that kind of stress herself. Slight dizziness and a headache that could be caused by her blood pressure being higher than normal. Chest pain… No. It was more like abdominal pain.

Cramps.

'Excuse me for just a minute,' she said. 'Talk amongst yourselves and come up with the types of situations you think you would struggle to cope with. I'll be right back.'

Except she wasn't. Jenna had to spend more than five minutes just sitting on that toilet seat, her head in her hands, breathing through the relief that she wasn't going to have to face the situation she'd known she could never deal with.

She wasn't pregnant.

And she'd never been so relieved in her entire life.

So why was it that, when she got back to her hotel room that evening, she could still feel like she hadn't shrugged off that weight of despair? Why did she feel a kind of grief, even, that she wasn't pregnant? This was crazy. So confusing that Jenna had to give up even thinking about it because it was too exhausting. She lay on the couch and closed her eyes, so drained that surely she would fall asleep and be able to escape in a matter of minutes.

She almost did. But it was in that space just before you fell asleep—that half-dream, half-reality space—that Jenna thought about Ollie. She could feel the weight of him falling asleep against her arm. She could smell that whiff of baby shampoo. And she could hear Mitch…that tone in his voice—not when he'd been so angry with her but way before that, the day that she'd found out he was a father and he'd been speaking to Ollie on the phone and she'd heard that note that had pierced her heart so sharply—the tone of a parent speaking to their precious child.

The sound of love.

Jenna opened her eyes as she felt the tears streaming down her face. She knew what the problem was, here. Despite a crippling fear that had made her avoid any kind of significant relationship in the last eight years and had made her believe that having another child was the last thing she would ever want, it had been nothing more than an extreme form of self-protection.

And it was a lie.

A baby would have been the best thing that could have happened for her.

A baby with a father like Andrew Mitchell would have been an absolute blessing.

Being a parent alongside Mitch—as partners, as *lovers*, perhaps even as husband and wife—would have made anything possible. Could have given her the courage to face all those fears.

Was it possible to feel something this big if it was only one-sided?

Was Jenna brave enough to try and find out?

This time, as her eyes drifted shut, Jenna knew she would be able to sleep peacefully. She had learned something about herself that, if nothing else, gave her hope in a future she hadn't known she'd wanted so much.

Was she brave enough to find out whether that was a possibility with Mitch? Whether what she'd thought she might have seen in his eyes that day, after they'd shared that butterfly's wing kiss, had been as real as the plans they had been making for a romantic getaway to a Greek Island.

Yes…but she needed to think about it. About how to do it. And that was when inspiration struck. When she got back to London, she needed to have a hunt in the glovebox of her vehicle. It was where she'd put that little blue car when she'd stumbled out of that restaurant having given Mitch enough time to carry Ollie well away from her.

Maybe it was still there.

Maybe Ollie might like it back?

CHAPTER ELEVEN

THE LITTLE BLUE car was sitting on the dashboard of the rapid response vehicle. Maybe that was why Ollie was the first thing to cross Jenna's mind when a Code Blue priority call came through on her radio to go to an incident with a critically ill child at the medical centre in Allensbury.

She was already past the outskirts of Greater London, on that side of the city, with her last call to a cyclist who had been knocked off her bike by a van in a village about halfway between Allensbury and Croydon. That patient was now being transported to a trauma centre by the helicopter that wouldn't be available to be dispatched to Allensbury for at least fifteen minutes.

Jenna was twenty minutes' drive away under legal speed limits but she knew she could do it in less than ten. She activated the siren and beacons with one hand as she pushed her responding button with the other. Then she pushed her accelerator to the floor. There was a hard knot in her belly that was rapidly getting bigger. Harder. It felt like fear. Was this fate trying to remind her of why she's been prepared to believe, for years and years, that she never wanted to be a mother again? Or a stepmother—especially to a child as adorable as Ollie?

A flash of blue caught in the periphery of Jenna's vision as she hurtled along in the fast lane of the motorway. Maybe it was just as well she hadn't quite found the courage to do something with that toy car in the few days since she'd been back from Ireland. This horrible fear couldn't be dismissed. Fear for Ollie. Fear for Mitch. And…yeah, fear for herself, even though she'd thought she'd kept herself safe from ever feeling fear like this again. If she'd needed any confirmation of just how deeply she cared for both Mitch and Ollie, this was it. This meant everything.

'Not Ollie,' she found herself whispering aloud. '*Please*…let it not be Ollie…'

But Ollie *was* the first person Jenna saw as she rushed through the front doors of Allenbury's medical centre a short time later. He was in the waiting room, on his grandfather's lap, and Michael Mitchell had his arms wrapped around the frightened looking child. He saw the alarm on Jenna's face but shook his head.

'Ollie's fine,' he told her quietly. 'Just scared. It's Mia that's sick.'

She didn't have to pause to try and give Ollie a reassuring smile and give his grandpa a nod of thanks for the information. Jenna kept moving, her arms full of the medical gear and drugs she was hoping she wouldn't need to use. The receptionist, with 'Josie' on her name tag, was pointing to a door.

'In here,' she urged Jenna. 'Dr Mitchell's with her. Her mum's here, now, too.'

It was Hanna who was sitting on the bed in Mitch's consulting room, in fact, but it was very clear that the patient was the small girl she was holding in her arms. Mia had a nebuliser mask on her face and Jenna could see what hard work it was for her to breathe. She was hunched forward, breathing at a rapid rate with her nostrils flaring, and she was using accessory muscles in her neck and chest. More worryingly, she looked very different to the happy little girl Jenna had seen rolling around and throwing grass at Pets' Day. This Mia was so lethargic, she was barely conscious. She didn't even look up when Jenna arrived.

Mitch did look up as she entered his consulting room and that first shared glance set the pattern for a current of non-verbal communication that did nothing to undermine what needed to happen here for Mia but did everything to let Jenna know she was in the right place at the right time for more than professional reasons.

I'm so glad you're here, Mitch's gaze told her.

I'm so glad I'm here, too.

Mitch's tone was calm as he spoke aloud. 'Mia was playing at home with Ollie after school. This could be an exercise-induced asthma attack although Hanna said she's had a bit of a runny nose for a day or two so it might be something viral. She didn't respond to repeated doses of her inhaler so Dad brought her in fast. Currently, she's tachycardic, tachypnoeic and breath sounds are decreasing despite the nebuliser. I'm about to get IV access.'

He already had a tourniquet around a tiny arm. Jenna knew it wasn't going to be easy to find a small vein in such dark skin but also knew that Mitch's confidence in being about to achieve a result was not misplaced.

His glance was adding something else, however. *I'm really worried. Mia's not doing well. We both know how quickly a severe asthma attack can become life-threatening.*

Jenna nodded. 'We could try some intramuscular adrenaline if there's any delay with getting access.' She held his gaze for a heartbeat. *We're a good team, Mitch. We've got this.*

Mia didn't make a sound as the small needle pierced her skin. She was looking up at her mother, holding her gaze fiercely. And Hanna was cuddling her, making the kind of soothing sounds mothers always made when comforting their child.

'You're doing a great job, Hanna,' Mitch told her. 'It's helping a lot.'

Hanna simply nodded and Jenna could understand how she might not be able to find any words. How terrified she probably was. As she finished adding a bronchodilator to the nebuliser mask's chamber to keep up the continuous mist of medication to be inhaled, she touched Hanna's arm, catching her glance to let her know she agreed with

Mitch—and that she understood exactly how hard this was.

Mitch was securing the IV line. 'I'll give an IV salbutamol bolus. And could you draw up some hydrocortisone for me, please?'

Jenna nodded. She'd noticed that Mia's lips were starting to look blue when she'd lifted the mask to fill the medication chamber. Mitch had a fleeting glance for her as she reached for the drug ampoule.

I know how hard this is for you, too. I'm sorry, Jenna...

It's okay... I'm fine.

'She's so drowsy.' Hanna's couldn't hide how afraid she was. 'Is she losing consciousness? How can we get her to hospital in time?'

'The helicopter will be on its way now,' Jenna assured her. 'And it's great they can land just across the road on the common. In the meantime, Mitch and I have got more that we can do to help.'

'Please help her...' It was no more than a desperate whisper. *'Please...'*

Minutes flashed past because there was so much to do. Listening to Mia's chest as her lung sounds got alarmingly quiet. Getting electrodes on to monitor her heart rate and rhythm. Monitoring her blood pressure and oxygen saturation. Administering more drugs. Thinking about what they didn't want to discuss out loud yet—that if Mia's condition continued to deteriorate they might have to go to what was a last resort of intubating and manually ventilating her and that carried a very real risk of complications. Death, even.

This time, it was Jenna that needed the silent reassurance when she glanced towards Mitch and she got it instantly.

We've got this, Jenna... You and me...

If Jenna hadn't been there with him, it would have been too hard to hold on to that confidence as the tension escalated, let alone to have enough to share. Thank goodness Mitch had recognised the severity of the situation as soon as Michael had run into the medical centre with Mia in his arms and he'd called for help. Thank goodness, by some extraordinary stroke of luck, Jenna had been dispatched and had been able to arrive in a remarkably short period of time. And thank goodness managing this life-threatening asthma attack didn't have to include intubating Mia.

In the last minutes before the air rescue crew arrived at the medical centre, their young patient's condition started to improve. By the time the intensive care flight medics were in the room and taking over to transport both Mia and her mother to a specialist paediatric hospital, the little girl was a lot more awake and, while her breathing was still too fast and laboured, she wrapped her arms around Hanna's neck as she was lifted and even found a smile.

Hanna also managed to find one.

'Love you, baby girl,' she said. 'We're going for a ride in a helicopter. That'll be something to tell Daddy about later, won't it?'

It was controlled chaos moving the stretcher with two occupants, IV set-up and bag of fluids and all the monitoring gear and attachments swiftly and smoothly out of the medical centre, across the road and into the helicopter. Jenna's vehicle was also parked on the Allensbury Common side of the road. Mitch was helping her carry some of her equipment back to her vehicle and a couple of officers from the local police were making sure bystanders were keeping a safe distance from the helicopter.

His father and Ollie were amongst those

bystanders, standing on the footpath, hand in hand, not far from Jenna's car, and Mitch saw the moment that Jenna was caught by the fear on Ollie's face. She dropped the backpack she was carrying on the footpath and crouched, holding out her arms. And Ollie let go of his grandfather's hand and ran to Jenna, hurling himself into those waiting arms and then clinging to her like a little monkey as his voice hitched and wobbled.

'Is Mia going to come back?'

'It's okay, Ollie. I know how scary it is but she's feeling better already and the people in the helicopter are taking really, really good care of her.'

Mitch was looking at those two dark heads so close together and their total focus on each other in this moment of seeking and offering comfort and his own heart felt like it was about to burst. It was hard to tell where the boundary was between where his love for Ollie finished and his love for Jenna began. Maybe there was no boundary. They were distinct parts but inseparable from the picture being created here.

A family picture.

Ollie didn't notice him stepping closer, putting down the gear he'd been carrying.

'But when can she come and play with me again?' he was asking.

'The doctors will want to look after her for a wee while,' Jenna told him. 'They might want to try some new puffers and medicine to see if they can stop something like this happening again.'

The rotors of the helicopter were picking up speed and the noise level was increasing but Mitch was close enough to still hear what Jenna was saying.

'How 'bout if I go and see Mia as soon as I can and I'll text Daddy to let him know how she is and then he can tell you?'

Mitch stepped even closer. 'I might go to the hospital myself very soon and see Mia and her mummy.'

He caught Jenna's gaze and was doing his best to convey a private message.

We need to talk. Please...asap.

'That's a great idea,' Jenna said. But her gaze was also responding.

Yes...there's so much we need to talk about.

'Can I come too?' Ollie raised his voice. The question was for his father but it was his grandfather on his other side who answered.

'We'll stay here, Ollie. I think your daddy

and Jenna can look after everything all by themselves.' Michael was smiling quietly as he looked from Mitch to Jenna—as if he'd heard that silent exchange they'd just shared.

Perhaps Ollie heard an undercurrent to what was actually being said, as well. He still had his arms wrapped around Jenna's neck but he unfurled one to reach out to his father. He still looked pale and worried and Mitch could see in his eyes a plea for touch. Closeness. The comfort of knowing you had someone who loved you enough to make the world a better place.

And then his gaze shifted a fraction to catch Jenna's and he could swear that he saw an identical plea in *her* eyes and Mitch could actually feel some jagged pieces in his soul shift a little. Enough that things were settling into place. A new place, perhaps, but that was okay. Better than okay.

He crouched down so that Ollie could wrap that free arm around his neck. He still had Jenna caught by his other arm so the most natural thing in the world was for Mitch to put his arm around Jenna as well. A group hug. They could feel the vibration of the helicopter's rotors gaining enough speed to lift off and the sound was covering any voices but it seemed like Mitch could hear what Jenna was saying as she suggested that Ollie should wave because Mia might be able to see him watching. As Ollie raised both arms to wave, she smiled at Mitch. He couldn't hear her now but he could lip read her words so easily.

'All good?'

Now it felt like there was hope that everything was going to work out in the best way possible. For Mia and her family. For his family, too. Ollie and his dad, himself and Jenna. He smiled back.

'Couldn't be better.'

They met in the observation ward next to the emergency department of the paediatric hospital.

Mia was sitting up in bed, eating ice cream. Her parents were sitting on opposite sides of the bed but holding hands across it. Hanna was brushing a tear from her cheek as she told Jenna about the enormous relief that Mia hadn't needed to be taken to the intensive care unit—that she had improved enough to be only staying to be monitored overnight and then she would be able to go home, as Mitch came in to stand beside Jenna. He'd heard enough to know all was well.

'That's great news.' He smiled. 'I'll have a chat to the doctors tomorrow. I'm thinking we might need a new action plan for Mia.'

Hanna nodded. 'They want to get all the results of the tests they've done this afternoon and they said they'll go over the plan with all of us. I'm so glad you came in, Mitch. I don't know how to thank you for what you did this afternoon. And you, Jenna.' She had to brush away another tear. 'You have no idea what it means…'

Mitch's gaze locked with Jenna's. 'Oh, I think we do,' he said quietly. It looked like it was an effort to break the eye contact. 'That looks like yummy ice cream, Mia.'

'Mmm…' Mia had ice cream over both cheeks and her chin.

'Ollie's going to be so happy to hear that you're feeling better. Hey…why don't we call him so he can say "hi" himself?'

The benefits of technology meant that it was only seconds before the two children could see each other on a phone screen and it was so lovely to see that wide grin on both their faces that Jenna had to swallow a rather big lump in her throat.

'Will you get me an ice cream on the way home, Daddy?' Ollie asked. 'A big one, like Mia's?'

'I think you'll be asleep by the time I get home,' Mitch told him. 'I'm going to take Jenna out to dinner first.'

Ollie's clear voice made all the adults smile. 'Because she's your girlfriend?'

'I think so…' Mitch said.

He was smiling at Ollie on the phone but his gaze was on Jenna and the question in his eyes was unmistakeable. She caught her bottom lip between her teeth as she nodded. Just once, but it was enough.

'Yeah,' he added. 'Because Jenna's my girlfriend.'

Perhaps it was because they had such big things to talk about that neither Jenna nor Mitch wanted to be enclosed in a restaurant. It was a pleasantly warm evening, so they began walking in the direction of Hyde Park to look for a takeout meal and, when they saw the familiar signage of the fast food outlet, it felt like a circle was being completed. Their relationship had ended at another branch of this same restaurant so maybe it was the perfect segue into forging something new.

Something better?

'I don't suppose you ever eat junk food like this normally, do you?'

'Only sometimes.' Jenna felt her heart squeeze as she remembered Ollie telling her that. 'And I think this might well be a "sometime".'

'Do you want to eat here or go into the park?'

'I'd love the park.'

'Same. What would you like to eat?'

'Surprise me.'

Mitch was back with a large paper bag in no time and a minute or two later they'd found a bench just inside the park grounds, with a lovely view of grass and huge trees and…squirrels.

'They'll take that hamburger out of your hands if you don't eat it fast enough,' Mitch warned.

His eyes were dancing with amusement and something else. Something huge that told her he didn't want to be anywhere else in the world right now. Or with anybody else. Which was exactly how she was feeling herself and her heart was so full that, curiously, she wasn't very hungry any longer. She broke off a piece of the bun for her hamburger and held it out. Sure enough, a bold squirrel ran forward to pluck it from her hand, which made them both laugh. Then they looked at each other and the laughter faded instantly but neither of them looked away.

'I love you, Jenna,' Mitch said softly.

'I love you, too,' she whispered.

Mitch didn't seem to be hungry any longer, either. He put the hamburger he was holding down on the bench beside him and didn't even notice the squirrels that appeared from nowhere and stole it because he was so focused on Jenna.

'Really? Oh, my God… I hoped so but… but I didn't dare let myself believe…'

'Same…'

It was Jenna that discarded the food in her hands completely this time but she wasn't aware of anything other than the way Mitch was looking at her. The way his hand came up to cup her chin and cheek. The way he touched her lips with his own with that gentle whisper of a kiss that was becoming her favourite thing in the world—a promise of what was to come next. And, yes, the 'real' kiss that followed took her straight into another world. One that only she and Mitch inhabited. Where time stopped. Where anything that wasn't good could be put aside for the moment, with the knowledge that when they went back into the 'real' world, it would be easier to cope with, because they would be coping together.

Maybe it was a vague awareness that they weren't alone by any means in this park that pulled them back to reality. Or maybe it was the squirrel that ran along the back of the bench in search of more food. Not that they pulled apart entirely. Jenna's head rested in the hollow beneath Mitch's collar bone. He tilted his head so that it rested on hers.

'I was going to call you,' he said softly. 'I was just waiting for the right moment. I'm not at all happy that Mia got so sick, of course, but I can't tell you how happy I was to see you again.'

'I was so scared when that call came through,' Jenna told him. 'My first thought was that something had happened to Ollie.'

'He was that scared as well. He adores Mia.'

They sat in silence for a breath or two and Jenna soaked in the solid feel of Mitch's chest beneath her cheek. The steady thump of his heartbeat.

'I thought I was keeping myself safe, you know. Not letting anybody too close in my life. It was easy to avoid a relationship with a guy because I genuinely wasn't interested. Until I met you...'

'I get that.' Jenna could feel Mitch's head move against her own as he nodded. 'I felt the same way after Tegan. If I saw a woman even looking at me twice, I'd think, Can't you see that that's never going to happen? *Ever?* Having Ollie to focus on made it even less likely. It felt like a life-saver.'

'And I had Eli for a long time...' Jenna let her breath out in a sigh. 'Enough time to get through the worst of my grief over Stefan. It was a lot harder after I loss Eli, though. I might have been able to see an attractive man and not be remotely interested or affected but...seeing children and babies everywhere—that was something completely different. It was unbearable...'

Mitch's arms tightened around Jenna. 'Oh, I get that, too. I knew how big an ask it was for you to come to Pets' Day but I was *so* happy that you did. Because I thought it could be the first step towards something bigger. Something that I realised I wanted very, very much.' His voice cracked. 'A future with you.' He was pressing his lips to Jenna's hair. 'A family...'

She twisted her head enough to look up at him. So that she could see the truth of what he was saying aloud. And so that he could see the truth in her eyes.

'I wanted that too,' she whispered. 'And I really believed it could happen.' One day— soon—she'd confess how she'd felt when she'd thought she was pregnant, and how she'd felt when she'd found out she wasn't. But that could wait until an even more intimate moment. 'Then Ollie fell asleep when I was reading him that story and...' She had to clear her throat. 'And I could smell baby shampoo and then, when he said he had a mummy to watch him like Mia did...'

'Oh, darling.' Mitch's tone was raw. 'It can just be a tiny thing that triggers grief and, for that moment in time, it feels like the worst just happened yesterday, doesn't it?'

'I got scared,' Jenna admitted. 'It was just that moment, but I didn't think it would be possible to survive it happening again. And then you were angry with me and I totally understood why…' Her breath hitched. 'I'd hurt Ollie. I'd made him cry.'

'No…' Mitch was smiling at her. So tenderly that Jenna could feel her eyes filling up. 'You know what he told me?'

'No…what?'

'That he knew why you didn't want a cuddle. That it was because you were too sad.'

Jenna blinked. 'He's four years old. How could he possibly know something like that?'

Mitch's smile widened. 'He's smart, I guess.'

'Like his dad.' Jenna smiled back at Mitch. 'But why was he crying so much?'

'Apparently, he'd lost something he loved. A little blue car?'

'Oh…' Jenna sat up. 'I know exactly where that is. Maybe I should give it to you to take home for him?'

'No…' Mitch stood up and held out his hand to Jenna. 'I think you should give it to him yourself. You should come home.'

And Jenna took his hand and let him pull her to her feet. Pull her right back into his arms, before they started walking anywhere. For another one of those kisses that stopped coherent thought for as long as it lasted. There was time for a very clear thought in the heartbeat before their lips touched, however.

Jenna knew with absolute clarity that she would follow this man she loved so much anywhere he wanted to take her. But the best place she could possibly go with him was home. A home that she would share with Mitch. And Ollie. And his dad and Jet and maybe even another baby one day.

Their home.

The place she wanted to be in for the rest of her life.

Mitch held her gaze as he lifted his lips from hers and Jenna could see a promise that felt like one of those butterfly kisses. A promise of so much more to come.

'All good?'

Jenna swallowed what felt like it could be the last of a fear she'd lived with for too long.

'Couldn't be better...'

* * * * *